SMOKE THAT THUNDERS

SMOKE THAT THUNDERS

PJ REECE

THISTLEDOWN PRESS

Canadian Cataloguing in Publication Data

Reece, PJ, 1945–
Smoke that thunders
ISBN 1-895449-88-X
I. Title.
PS8585.E3477 S64 1999   C813'.54   C99-920043-7
PR9199.3.R419 S64 1999

Cover photograph of Victoria Falls by Gordon Donkin
Typeset by Thistledown Press Ltd.
Printed and bound in Canada

Thistledown Press Ltd.
633 Main Street
Saskatoon, Saskatchewan
S7H 0J8

Thistledown Press gratefully acknowledges the financial assistance of the Canada Council for the Arts, the Saskatchewan Arts Board, and the Government of Canada through the Book Publishing Industry Development Program for its publishing program.

ACKNOWLEDGMENTS

I may have written this story but others coaxed it out of me. Jack Silberman, for one, who saw it as a motion picture. Harold Tichenor who wanted to read it as a novel. Vince Hemingson, writing buddy and coffee mate, who unleashed his critical red pen upon an early draft. Thanks to Pamela Ann McGarry for her comments and enthusiasm through the rewrites. And to my parents who never discouraged me from setting out on any of my adventures.

The Harold Greenberg Fund kept the wolf from my door while I wrote early drafts of this story in script form. And thanks, finally, to Susan Musgrave, my editor, for being a different kind of wolf at my door. Her notes kept me prisoner through a process that taught me much about the craft of writing.

for my father

ONE

Do you have a confirmation number, sir?"
The ticket agent had punk red hair that clung to her temples like flames licking up a wall.

David turned for one last desperate glimpse of Jackie as she rushed away into the airport crowd, then glanced at the pictures she'd thrown at him, a strip of self-portraits taken at a photo booth.

"Confirmation number, sir?" The agent studied him over reading glasses as he held the photos in his mouth so that he could withdraw two passports bound by an elastic band from his mother's shoulder bag.

"Sorry." He spat out the pictures. "All I have is a name. Livingstone." He handed her the passports. The photos left a taste in his mouth, like vinegar.

"Livingstone, Livingstone, Livingstone." She typed it in. "We show only one reservation — for a Barbara Livingstone."

"That's her." David lifted a suitcase onto the scale. "Toronto. Returning on Monday. She wants an aisle seat."

"I'm afraid seat selection is take-what-you-get at this time."

"She said she won't take no for an answer."

"Oh?" said the agent.

"Yeah, my mom's a lawyer."

"A lawyer, oh, my," the agent said. "In that case we'd better put her in the captain's seat. Now what about the other one?"

The other one? David picked the second passport off the counter and opened it. It was his. His mother kept them together for safekeeping.

"And the other one?" The agent kept typing.

David looked at the blue General Motors VISA card his mother had shoved in his hand before running off to make an important phone call.

"Going once, going twice . . . " The Air Canada Mademoiselle affixed a baggage tag to the handle of the suitcase and hauled it onto the conveyor behind her.

David heard a boarding announcement for Saskatoon but it came to him through the airport din sounding like sex-and-death. So, Jackie's little peace offering hadn't appeased him, not even her confession that she still loved him. It wasn't enough and he didn't know why. He only knew that he was burning up.

"Going three times," she said.

"Yeah," said David. "The other one would be me." He slapped the credit card and passport on the counter.

"Hmmm," she said, "David Livingstone. There's a famous name."

"That's what they say."

"Toronto for you as well?"

"No."

"Well?"

"Darkest Africa."

ð» ð» ð»

"Ladies and gentlemen, in preparation for landing please
fasten your seat belts and return your seats and trays to the
upright position."

David Livingstone woke up sweating. It was daylight.
He'd been dreaming. In his nightmare, Africa had no
straight lines. Why that should cause him panic, he had no
idea. He raised the blind to find the 747 banking into its
final approach for landing. He turned to the wide-awake
flight steward sitting beside him blocking his escape.
Corvette red lipstick discoloured one of her front teeth.
"Smudge" he wanted to call her.

"I thought I asked you to wake me."

"You needed the sleep," she said. "You want to be a
wreck when you get home?"

David swallowed against a curt reply and smiled. Since
Interpol in London had radioed the Captain that a
runaway was on board, he had received special attention
up there thirty-three thousand feet over the Sahara Desert.
Although he was under some kind of house arrest, the
cabin crew had served him extra helpings of chicken
cordon bleu. Rumours spread throughout the plane that
a celebrity was on board, and who else could it be but him?
His denials only made fellow passengers more curious.
How difficult it must be to live with fame, some had said.
It had become embarrassing for him because the attendant
who guarded him knew the truth.

David undid his seat belt and got up but Smudge
wouldn't let him past. Not even to go to the toilet. She
said it was too late.

David sat down and turned to the window. Too late is right, he thought. Too late to worry. He gave himself up to a spectacular eagle's eye view of Tanzania and her villages, all daub and wattle, thatch and red mud. Huts down there were round and grouped in circles while the trails between them wandered like rivers. Maybe it was true. Maybe they hadn't heard of the straight line, after all.

"The temperature in Dar es Salaam this morning is a muggy thirty-seven degrees Celsius. Captain Pellegrini reminds you to remain in your seats until after we've landed and we've come to a complete stop in front of the terminal building."

The plane passed over little black people fishing from tiny boats on a chocolate brown river. Something else at the edge of the stream caused David's heart to jump and his head to bump the glass, something lean and tawny and cat-like. It vanished beneath the wing and all David could see was dusty green and rusty bush country that gave way to a wasteland of gravel and concrete and rows of blue landing lights and a mile or two of straight, straight lines. David looked at his watch.

"I know. We're five minutes early," said Smudge. "Captain Pellegrini, he's a bit of a maverick. I hope he uses landing gear this time." She winked.

David cinched up his seat belt. "You're dead if you do and dead if you don't," he said. He saw the sparkle in her eye turn cold and critical, which had the effect of turning his cynicism on himself and the way he presented himself to the world — hair cropped short like a recruit, stubble he'd recently let grow on his chin because, curiously, it grew in red, a black T-shirt, European, cost him sixty-five bucks because no other style sported a neck large enough to expose the collar bone which he thought kind of sexy. He became self conscious of his attitude, cocksure by all reports, that was wearing thin. He sensed the scar under his lip where the hockey stick had sliced through to the gum killing the nerves in two teeth. The sight of blood had disgusted Jackie but had impressed his buddies, an epiphany that opened David's eyes to the fact that women and men march to different drummers. Since then he'd come to realize that most girls didn't march at all. They meandered like rivers, like tourists without itineraries.

As the plane touched down, Smudge advised him that they would disembark together and suggested that it would be a good idea to apologize to everyone to whom he was introduced. "And you'll be on a plane home before you know it." She smiled, exposing her red tooth.

He felt sorry for her, yet he turned away. He couldn't afford to let anything hijack his emotions, not for the next few minutes.

One by one, passengers moved through the exit, out of stale British Air into an atmosphere that was muggy and sweet. David paused at the top of the stairs to fill his lungs. He saw five armed guards on the roof of the terminal building and a single soldier in green- and brown-bespattered battle gear waiting beside an open military Jeep at the bottom of the staircase.

"David?" Smudge nudged him from behind. "You're holding up the line."

In his mind's eye he could see her smile. She was not the enemy, he thought, but that smudge of hers was a public relations disaster.

"If I were you, I'd check your tooth," he said.

She pulled out a tissue, wiped the tooth and smiled for him again. When he nodded approval she blew him a discreet kiss, which gave him the courage to follow her down the steps. Smudge never looked back as the sergeant corralled him into the back seat of the Jeep between Mrs. Wilson, a compact woman "from the embassy" who looked as friendly as a roll of barbed wire, and Officer Mbele, a quiet woman with a gun.

"I needed this today like I need a hole in my head," said the Wilson woman, looking David over with obvious contempt. David examined her at the same time. She had gelled grey hair and nicotine fingers.

"No comment," said David.

"Don't test my patience, young man," she said as the Jeep accelerated across the tarmac. "Or we'll show you the inside of a Tanzanian jail."

"My mother's a lawyer, in case you want to know," he said.

"She sounded like the judge and jury when I talked to her an hour ago, young man," said Mrs. Wilson.

"I don't know what the big deal is," David said. "I'll pay her back."

"You can tell her as much on the phone," said Wilson. "After that, it's home the way you came. So, no more monkey business."

David focused on the Tanzanian flag that rippled over the hood of the Jeep — green, black, blue and yellow, as lush as the jungle.

Inside the arrivals hall, Wilson shoved her way to the front of a lineup where she presented David, along with his passport, to Mr. Tembo, an aging immigration official with a thick grey mustache and bulging eyes. He noticed a photo protruding from the passport, lodged in it like a bookmark,

"That witchy babe there," said David, "just ignore her."

Mr. Tembo pulled the photo out far enough to see a striking young lady with Meryl Streep cheek bones and hands buried in dark wavy hair at her temples. Her closed eyes suggested she had a headache or, more likely, the camera had caught her primping. Tembo pushed her down out of sight causing another pose to pop out the bottom. This time she nailed the lens with her best shot. Jacqueline Polanski was a knockout any way you looked at her. David snatched the strip of photos. Tembo chuckled, opened the passport, then fell grim once again.

"Livingstone?" he said. His eyes became suspicious slits. He slammed the passport shut and shoved it to the edge of the counter. "Go home," he said, arms crossed.

David appealed to Mrs. Wilson with a withering look that said, "Here we go with the old Dr. Livingstone thing again." His father had filled him in when he was a kid. More recently, Mr. MacGregor, his English teacher, had dredged it up in class: "1871, Henry Stanley, a reporter from the *New York Herald* searches Africa for the long-lost Scottish explorer, Dr. David Livingstone, and, upon tracking him to the shores of Lake Tanganyika, says by way of a greeting, 'Dr. Livingstone, I presume.'" Why that meaningless little comment should become legend is anybody's guess.

Tembo burst into laughter, then stopped short, his eyes slits once again.

"Entry forbidden!" he said.

Mrs. Wilson smiled through clenched teeth. "My dear Mr. Tembo — "

"Excuse me, Madame, I've always wanted to say that," Tembo said.

"He's going home, believe me," said Wilson, pushing the passport back at him.

Tembo hammered it with his stamp, chuckling all the while, then held it out to David like bait. Wilson grabbed the passport and pushed David through the turnstile.

Flanked by Wilson and Mbele, he moved through crowds of Africans toward the main terminal exit. He asked for a toilet break but Wilson insisted on proceeding to the embassy, twenty minutes away. Failure weighed on him like ten fathoms over a drowning man. Nausea rose like dough in his throat, as if his insides wanted no part of this surrender. Yet, he couldn't help but stare at the Tanzanians, most of them shiny and songful, some as colourful as a Kodak ad, some drab as dust. He stopped at a drinking fountain and splashed water on his face. It felt better with his head down, better still when he took a sip.

"For God's sake! We don't drink the water." Mrs. Wilson reprimanded Officer Mbele for not stopping him. David spit into the basin. It was so much like vomiting that he held his chest and swallowed, then held himself over the basin, breathing hard. Mrs. Wilson stemmed her impatience with a breath so high into her chest it puffed her up like a cobra. "Cuff him. I'll get him some lemonade," she said and marched off.

"Is this water, like, fatal?" he asked.

Mbele unhooked handcuffs from her belt. "To be sure," she said, grinning.

"Seriously, I feel it," said David. "I'm going to be sick."

Mbele took him by the hand and led him to the lavatory. David angled toward the men's room but she snapped the cuffs on one wrist and directed him into the women's. Every cubicle except one was occupied and it had a toilet that wouldn't quit running.

"You have to unhook me," said David.

Mbele looked once to make sure her boss was nowhere in sight, then unlocked the handcuffs. David closed the cubicle door and unzipped. As he urinated, he leaned forward and looked in the water tank. The rubber valve flopped about, freed from its moorings. He zipped up and re-established the stopper on its hinges. Too easy, he thought, all too easy. He undid his handywork with one yank.

"Mrs. Mbele! I could use an extra hand in here." When Mbele arrived at the cubicle door, David had both hands in the tank.

"I need you to hold one hinge in place while I work on the other one," he said. She reached into the toilet tank allowing the handcuffs to dangle from her wrist within the mechanical contraption. She told David to hurry, so he rattled the levers to maximum effect and told her he had only to connect the chain.

"Got it," he said, then stepped back, wiping his hands on his shirt.

"Mr. David. You have made a mistake. I am stuck. Mr. David! Where are you going? *Umekosa! Umekosa!*"

David made his way quickly toward the main entrance but stopped when he heard Wilson shout his name. He couldn't see her anywhere but guards at the entrance turned his way, on the alert, so he ran toward the check-in counters. A police whistle brought the bustling crowd to a halt, forcing David to melt into the closest queue. A middle-aged German couple fresh from safari took gruff exception to his butting in. David asked them if they were explorers. The very idea of it seemed to lend a delightful new interpretation to their holiday and they began to tell David about their harrowing encounter with Africa's most dangerous animal, the hippo, as Officer Mbele ran past with the plunger apparatus dangling from her wrist. A single police whistle became a chorus of whistles from every corner of the building. Hundreds of travellers scattered, crouched or flattened themselves on the floor as if terrorists had already opened fire. The human forest in which David hid fell like a clearcut leaving him in the open.

He darted towards the East African Airways counter, ducked beneath it and crawled over the luggage scales onto the moving conveyor where he rode between two cages of whining Rottweiler pups until he entered a hole in the wall and disappeared behind black rubber flaps into darkness.

TWO

There's an old saying that goes: a journey of a thousand miles begins with a single step. It's supposed to be encouraging. It's meant to roust you out of bed and onto your feet, to outwit your apathy and outfit you mentally for the road. It was good enough to encourage sixteen year old David Livingstone onto Air Canada flight #896 leaving Vancouver, Canada, at 4:55 p.m. direct for London Heathrow with an onward ticket on British Airways to Dar es Salaam. What it didn't include and should have, according to David, was a warning. It should have put a guy on notice that every step of the way his motives, once so urgent, would melt under even greater pressure. It might have warned him that his crises, negotiated one by one, could become stepping stones leading away from his goal to some deeper, darker dead end, or so he imagined as he let the conveyor take him the next step, into the baggage department.

Half a dozen handlers watched as David bailed from the conveyor belt and sprinted for a tractor train loaded with suitcases and automobile tires heading outside. He leapt aboard and crouched in a cavity of rubber and Samsonite.

While moving across the tarmac, David didn't dare look, but he couldn't close his ears against the clip-clop of troops mobilizing on concrete.

The luggage train stopped. David raised his head to find himself in the shadow of a Zambian Airways Lockheed 10-11. The tractor driver began loading suitcases onto the conveyor leading into the belly of the plane. He saw soldiers fanning out from the terminal entrance, bayonets protruding from barrels of rifles held diagonally across their chests. Two soldiers ran up the staircase into the plane. One of them glanced at the luggage buggies parked below.

"*Mzungu!*" he cried.

David leapt into the tractor driver's seat, turned the key and accelerated beneath the plane in the direction of the bush on the far side of the runway. He heard a gunshot and looked over his shoulder. A single-engine Apache surprised him as it taxied toward him from the other direction. David swerved, the buggies jackknifed, and two carts tipped sending the load of Goodyears rolling helter skelter across five acres of runway. Soldiers poured over the baggage train, shouting, as they dumped the rest of the luggage in search of the runaway. They ignored the tires, however, one of which rolled to a stop near a row of parked single-engine Cessnas.

David emerged from the hollow of the truck tire like a snail from its shell and sprinted for cover between two of the aircraft. He pulled on doors until he found one unlocked, the pilot's door of a white, high-winged Cessna 182. He hunkered down behind the front seats where he tried to catch his breath. His only escape from the sounds of combat boots on concrete was into wishful thinking, as he extracted the passport from under his belt and took refuge in the image of God's gift to romantically-challenged young men, Jackie Polanski. This time he read the photo differently. Hands at her temples suggested shock, maybe even shame for her role in his splitting so suddenly. There was no doubt in David's mind that she would be struggling to explain his behaviour. The David she knew was hardly the impulsive type. The David she knew was the master of minimalist style, the smug heir to his grandfather's Scotch whisky fortune — on the condition that he serve five years in the armed forces or five in a monastery. "Take your choice, Laddy." He could afford to talk himself out of anything, Jackie had told him. So, where were his half-baked survival philosophies when he needed them most? *Don't leave home — with or without it!* He'd become famous in the halls of Kitsilano High for that one. It should have kicked in as he stepped up to the ticket counter with his mother's credit card. *Dead if you do, dead if you don't*, was another Livingstone classic. It had more cachet than *Fiat Lux*, the school's motto — Let there be light.

"The Lord above made man to help his neighbour . . ."

It was a man's voice, singing. "No matter where, on land or sea or foam . . ."

A soldier interrupted the song with a request for permission to search the plane for a "*mzungu*". That word again, thought David. What did it mean? It sounded like an insect, something incessant and annoying, something that should be crushed.

"I haven't got him up my sleeve, my good man," said the man. The accent sounded Oxford and the voice deep and rich, the words coming out warm and whipped with a measure of goodwill.

"Yes, sir!" The soldier snapped his heels and ran off.

"The Lord above made man to help his neighbour . . . "

The man resumed singing as he opened the Cessna door and seated himself behind the controls. "And with a little bit of luck, with a little bit of luck, when he comes around you won't be home . . . "

He switched on the magnetos and set the mixture to rich. He was a large black man, around fifty, in a suit as dark and sleek as slate. David looked for cufflinks, expecting gold or diamonds, but they weren't showing. What he saw instead were vicious scars on the back of the man's right hand. David couldn't believe the man hadn't seen him.

"With a little bit, with a little bit, with a little bit of bloomin' luck." The singing pilot finished with a flourish and looked at his watch. "Damn it all," he said, then flipped more switches. "A little more punctuality! A little more attention to the common weal. To God and country, by Jove."

The man turned the ignition key. The single engine started up with a roar, then a shiver and a shake that reverberated right through David who cowered behind his seat. The singing started again, this time, "Get Me to the Church on Time!" He taxied toward the runway with an earphone pressed against his right ear and the microphone at his lips.

"Dar Tower, this is Cessna Fiver Hotel Charlie Alpha Tango." The pilot paused to listen. "Say again, old chap. Requesting takeoff clearance." He tried another radio channel. "I can't understand a bloody word you're saying!" he said. "Speak the Queen's English or not at all." He chucked the headset into the back seat, withdrew a log book from a pocket in the door and reading glasses from his breast pocket and jotted down some notes.

David could hear the control tower through the earphones that lay inches from his head. The tone of voice sounded urgent so he drew the headset toward him.

"That's a negative, Charlie Alpha Tango. Hold your position. I repeat, hold your position. All flights are temporarily suspended. Acknowledge, over."

The scarred hand flipped switches and turned knobs that tested magnetos, flaps, fuel, and rpms as David listened to the air traffic controller who spoke no longer in the clipped language of international air space.

"Mr. Ngoma, sir? There's a security alert, I'm afraid. We're shutting down. Do you read me? Sir, do you read me? Acknowledge, please."

David lifted his head to see why the Cessna had stopped at the threshold of the runway. It was all clear. Behind them, a dozen soldiers approached on the run, only fifty yards away. David turned to see Mr. Ngoma squinting into the bright sky in both directions.

"Baby, you can drive my car; Baby, you can be a star . . . "

David looked again to see the soldiers advancing like a wave at the turning of the tide. He opened his mouth to speak, to say something, to hell with the consequences, when Mr. Ngoma pushed in the throttle and the mechanical racket drowned out anything David might have said. The plane lurched forward onto the runway, swung ninety degrees and accelerated.

David glanced one last time at soldiers so close behind the plane they could have spit on the tail wing. Through the gap between the two front seats he saw the speedometer pass through fifty to sixty miles per hour. When it reached sixty-five, Saint Ngoma pulled back on the control stick. The airframe pounded David's ribs until a higher frequency buzz signalled they were airborne.

The engine continued to roar while everything else about life melted smooth as sleep. This was the kind of peace David imagined he'd find on the day Jackie was finally his, not just because she said she loved him, but because when he returned from far-flung adventures he would be bursting with mysteries that, for reasons he did not yet understand, seemed to attach themselves to individuals who travel solo. On that day, he would choose her.

THREE

"It seemed to me as if I also were buried in a vast grave full of unspeakable secrets. I felt an intolerable weight oppressing my breast, the smell of damp earth, the unseen presence of victorious corruption, the darkness of an impenetrable night . . . "

David remembered well the series of events that set his brain to boil, starting with Mr. MacGregor standing at the corner of his desk at the front of the class cradling that leather-bound first edition of Joseph Conrad's *Heart of Darkness*. MacGregor and his khaki shirt complete with epaulettes and pencil slots, his heavy-duty bush pants with pockets large enough to hold hand grenades, and a silver belt buckle in the shape of a character from the Chinese alphabet. Jackie had looked it up before MacGregor himself had enlightened the class. "Crisis", it meant.

Rumours rampant in the school's hallways pegged James MacGregor as some kind of mercenary soldier gone to seed. Lucky for him that the regular Grade Nine English teacher had recently won herself a seat in the provincial election and was now the Minister of Education. David and his classmates couldn't decide if this was a blessing or a curse. Only Jacqueline Polanski paid rapt attention to the six-foot-two Mr. MacGregor as he read on.

"The fact is, I was completely unnerved by a sheer blank fright, pure abstract terror, unconnected with any distinct shape of physical danger."

For someone reading, MacGregor didn't spend much time looking at the page. Clearly, he knew this opus by heart, which made it easier for him to see the note being passed around the room and which brought stifled chuckles at each pit stop. Mr. MacGregor must have known who authored the note because when it returned to David's desk he walked down the aisle toward him, still reading.

" . . . as if something altogether monstrous, intolerable to thought and odious to the soul had been thrust upon me unexpectedly," MacGregor read on.

David passed the note to Jackie across the aisle but it fell from her desk. He reached for it with the point of his lizard-skin cowboy boot but MacGregor beat him to it. He pinned it to the floor with his brushed leather Kodiak boot leaving David bending over into an extreme close up of that Chinese belt buckle.

MacGregor picked up the note and, without breaking narrative stride, returned to the blackboard where he took a piece of chalk and wrote, "Detention", and under it, "David Livingstone". MacGregor quit reading, closed the book and spoke David's full name as if it sat on a pedestal. "David Livingstone."

No one knew what MacGregor had in mind, but they all knew how he could hold you up to the light for examination. "Stand up, Livingstone."

It was like High Noon except that MacGregor had all the ammo. He possessed the note, but more than that he had the unfair advantage of all of English Literature on his side.

David brushed eraser filings off his T-shirt as he stood up. He stuffed his hands in the back pockets of his heavy-gauge Diesel jeans.

"I'm sorry," he said. "It was thrust upon me unexpectedly, I swear. Odious it was, too." This earned a chuckle from everyone, including a smile from Mr. MacGregor.

"I presume you all know," MacGregor said, "that Dr. David Livingstone was an extraordinarily brave man." MacGregor picked up the novel again. "Like Marlow, Conrad's hero, Dr. Livingstone explored Africa — what they once called the Dark Continent. In 1855, he discovered, as we used to say, Victoria Falls. You knew that, didn't you, Dr. — I mean, David Livingstone?"

David never wanted to be tested on the details, but he knew enough. He knew that imperialism was a thing of the past. You couldn't go around like Christopher Columbus any more, discovering America, or like Anthony Henday discovering the Rocky Mountains and claiming it all for your king and country. It was bad enough being a white male these days without the added burden of having to live down the ego-maniacal exploits of some hundred and fifty year old colonial do-gooder.

"You must be proud of such a name," continued Mr. MacGregor. "My name is MacGregor. Not a bad name, but not like Livingstone! The very name could lend one a mission in life. Am I right?"

David shrugged. He knew Livingstone had been a missionary, if that's what he meant.

"Not to mention — courage! Am I right?"

David lapped up MacGregor's ironic praise. The class fed on his folly like a pride of hungry lions. Jackie, too, David noticed, except she wasn't smirking. She crossed her arms and looked out the window as if she was remembering, very clearly, yesterday.

They had spent the unseasonably warm autumn Sunday afternoon with their friends, Noel and Dak, at Lion's Bay, less than an hour's drive up the coast. After parking at the marina, they walked back up the steep road to the railway tracks that hugged the cliff, then hiked the rails for fifteen minutes, stopping only once before they reached the top of the granite wall that fell seventy feet into Howe Sound. David warned Jackie that if she mentioned Mr. MacGregor one more time they'd leave her tied to the tracks.

Noel and Dak had stripped to their skivvies and were over that cliff holding hands before David had removed his sunglasses. Jackie had undressed down to a white T-shirt over a two-piece cobalt bathing suit. It was enough to start David stripping but he stopped when he felt like a sailor being lured by a siren onto the rocks. He was in no hurry to kill himself and he told Jackie so. Dak and Noel were still alive, she'd replied. Fine, he'd said, with Dak and Noel, what you saw was what you got. He'd implied that he was different. The implication was that he had history.

No one knew how it had affected him, the mystery surrounding his father's disappearance five years ago, and no one had the nerve to ask. The facts were that in the early morning following a car rally in which Errol Livingstone placed third, he went for a drive up this same tortuous mountain highway, continued past Lion's Bay toward Squamish and Whistler and never returned. Rumours proliferated like cockroaches, stories of accidents, amnesia, even suicide, until two years later a team of German kayakers found his remains while dragging the depths for one of their own. Both Errol and the freulein were caught in a deep eddy at the bottom of the pool at the foot of a thirty foot waterfall in Garibaldi Park. Errol, or what remained of him, had been swirling around down there for a long, long time. The park warden had said he might have remained there forever.

Without being bitter about it, David's mother used her dead husband as a bad example for David's own good. Barbara kept criticizing Errol for "not living his passion". Being a coward is what she'd meant. He had a fear of flying, literally. It killed any chance he might have had of taking his rally career to the limit. She said he was killing himself slowly, spending his life as a mailman delivering postcards from the four corners of the earth, tales of adventure he should have been writing, himself. It had occurred to David that his mother may have driven his father to the deep end, if not all the way over the edge.

David watched Jackie skip toward the precipice, catapult into the air with arms spread and drop like a spear into blue-black water.

"Come, be bold, David Livingstone."

Mr. MacGregor handed him the note and a piece of chalk and invited him to use the broad expanse of blackboard to come clean, to risk dissolving the boundary between his private thoughts and public persona. David would never admit as much but he found this razor's edge of risk attractive. He double-checked the note.

"David! David! David!" the class shouted.

While David inched toward the blackboard, MacGregor drew the class's attention to his Chinese belt buckle. Crisis was two characters in one, he showed them — the top one, danger, the bottom one opportunity. It meant, "the point of decision".

"To benefit from crisis, you must first survive it," MacGregor said.

At the sound of the noon buzzer the class groaned. David made a show of wiping sweat off his brow, but MacGregor, with hands raised, kept the lid on. He waited one more beat to see if David would oblige, then brought his hands down like a conductor ending the symphony. The class broke in with a chorus of "Boos!". MacGregor took the note out of David's hand and threatened to read it aloud. Jackie covered her eyes.

"Would you buy a used car from this guy?"

The class shrieked, laughing no longer at MacGregor, however, but with him and his infinite good nature. David retreated red-faced to his desk where Jackie stood ready to leave, holding her heavy English anthology to her breast.

"Come, be bold, David Livingstone," she said, mimicking MacGregor.

"Easy for you to say," he said.

"You're right. I'm sorry," she said. "How insensitive of me." She glanced at MacGregor who continued to chuckle over that note, then she looked David in the eye and said, "It must be much more difficult to actually be a man."

David watched her head for the door, then stop as MacGregor raised his voice again.

"As for your curious question — we might well discover the answer. I have a '53 Merc for sale. A two-door rag top. If anyone's interested, see me Saturday. Corner of Crown and 27th."

Jackie said something to MacGregor, something he leaned close to hear. Was she placing first dibs on the car, David wondered, or giving him her phone number? As she left the room without looking back, MacGregor crumpled the note and launched it toward the waste basket half a room away. Bingo.

"I'm getting married in the morning . . . " Mr. Ngoma was still at it, singing, "Get Me to the Church on Time".

David felt so sure he'd been seen that he let down his guard and lifted his head enough to look out the window, then inched himself vertical for a view of the ground and what appeared to be a herd of animals — thousands, if not millions of them — streaming across a vast plain. They resembled a hungry-looking hybrid of buffalo and cow. David sat up in the back seat. What more did he have to do to get caught?

"Wildebeest!" said Ngoma without turning around. "Migrating! Now, young man, where would you like out?"

Ngoma had throttled back the engine in level flight so that there was no doubt about what he'd said, yet David wanted to see Ngoma's lips move before he committed to an answer.

"Next stop, Morogoro!" said Ngoma turning his head, showing David his profile. "End of the line!"

"How about Victoria Falls?" said David.

"Victoria Falls!" Ngoma bellowed.

David was glad he hadn't caused the man a heart attack.

"You mean, Mosi-O-Tunya," said Mr. Ngoma.

"Mossy-O'Tuna?" said David.

"No, no — Mo-see-O-Tooonya! Say it correctly, if you don't mind."

Mzungu heads for Mosi-O-Tunya, thought David. He was learning the language. "Doesn't anyone call it Victoria Falls anymore?" he asked.

Ngoma laughed again as he set the plane into a sudden dive, punishment, David thought, for mentioning "Victoria Falls". What would Ngoma do if he found out his name was Livingstone?

"Mosi-O-Tunya!" yelled Ngoma. "Smoke that thunders!"

David reached behind him for a seat belt. "How come you didn't turn me in back there?" he asked.

"I love a good story and I'm betting you have one!" said Ngoma. He had to yell to be heard.

"I don't think so. Unless you think stealing your mother's credit card is high adventure."

"When I was your age I borrowed a Vespa without asking and drove to the big city!" said Ngoma. "I had heard wondrous things of the outside world. Europe, America! I stayed in Dar a week in the hope of seeing a film. I stole my way through a stage door into *The Sound of Music*. It changed my entire life!"

"That's exactly why I'm here," said David.

"Say again, old chap!"

"To change my entire life!" yelled David.

"So, you see! I have saved your life!"

David didn't feel saved, not in the larger sense of the word, but he had to admit that he hadn't felt so optimistic since he left Vancouver.

"Thank you very much," he said. "My name's Livingstone."

Ngoma turned his fat neck far enough around so that David could see the whites of both dark eyes.

"David Livingstone," David said.

Ngoma pulled hard on the control stick, launching them into a steep climb that brought the Cessna to a stall. A piercing alarm announced the end of forward motion. The plane slid backwards before the nose dropped like a rock and the plane plummeted in a spiralling dive. Ngoma started singing again while David felt his stomach trying to bail out through the trap door of his big mouth.

FOUR

N ose down, my boy. Left rudder. Left foot!"
Ngoma kept his fingers lightly on the control stick as
David, who had been invited to climb into the front seat
and take over at a set of dual controls, brought the plane
in askew over the grass runway. Ngoma pushed in the
throttle and pulled back on the stick so that the engine
roared and the plane rose into the sky again.

David looked down upon a ranch-style house with a
roof of red tiles. He saw a black man in a white jacket and
green woollen toque standing by the windsock, cradling a
fire extinguisher in his arms. David wasn't sure, but it
looked like he crossed himself.

"Remember, a plane takes off and flies by itself but it's
you who must set it down." Ngoma seemed pleased to
have a student. As he took the Cessna to a thousand feet
and circled for another approach, he reviewed the princi-
ples of flight. It made little sense to David until they were
soaring over the runway again and Ngoma handed control
to David and told him to "land like a bloody duck!"

"Nose up!" yelled Ngoma. "Not so much! Down!
Down!" Ngoma resisted taking over, commanding only

the throttle. When he pulled it all the way back the stall alarm shrieked again and the nose of the plane dropped like one end of a teeter totter and landed hard on the grass. They bounced into the air and landed crabwise again and skidded across slick grass toward the manservant who didn't know which way to run for his life.

The Cessna came to a stop adjacent the limp windsock.

"Wow! I landed," said David.

"That, my boy, I would call a controlled crash. But, with a little bit of bloomin' luck, you'll be a pilot. Why not?"

David took a deep breath and looked out over rust-coloured fields that descended to a meandering green line of jungle a quarter of a mile away. Through the leaves a glint of sun reflected off what must have been a reach of water. Never-say-die sisal plants grew like weeds in fields around the long, low white house. Blood red bougainvillaea framed the doorway and ran along the eaves to a trellis that covered a patio and breezeway between two sections of the bungalow. On the brick-paved horseshoe courtyard sat a white, four-door Mercedes 560.

"Good God," said Ngoma, "The towel." He pointed to the servant who entered the house with a dishtowel draped over a forearm. Ngoma shut the plane down. "Dinner must be getting cold. Come quickly or Alex will be making us serve ourselves."

"Thanks anyway, Mr. Ngoma, but I've got to put some miles under my belt. How far is it to Mosi — to 'smoke that thunders'?"

"Better you first put some sustenance under that belt, my boy," said Ngoma. "Before you tackle the Hell Run."

"The Hell Run?" queried David.

"The highway. Fifteen-hundred miles into the heart of Zambia."

"Fifteen-hundred —?"

"Come, we will discuss everything."

David followed Ngoma to the house. Hell Run? MacGregor hadn't said anything about any Hell Run. On the way across the brick courtyard David ran his fingers along the hood of the Mercedes. He stopped to read a nameplate attached to the house beside the door, announcing the residence of "The Honourable Felix Fackson Ngoma, Minister of Highways, the United Republic of Tanzania."

Lunch awaited them on a coffee table on the patio. From there David could see the small river and it's cloak of jungle. Alex poured Tusker Premium into chunky beer mugs while David stuffed a dinner roll into his mouth. Ngoma raised his glass. "To one who marches to the beat of his own heart," he said.

"Thank you, sir," said David. "Everybody else thinks I'm on the run." He fed a celery stick into a full mouth, all the time focusing on those deep scars on the back of Ngoma's right hand.

"The heart is sometimes a fearful friend," said Ngoma. "The best policy is to take notice when it growls."

"Mine was growling, all right." David could hardly speak for a full mouth.

"Might have been your stomach," said Mr. Ngoma.

"It was all of me, trust me. Anti-social, that's what she called me."

"Well, well. Most people in your condition are seeking refuge in virtual reality these days, but David Livingstone chooses the real world. Tell me true, you are trying to prove something."

"Prove what?" said David, starting to burn again.

"Great adventures are born of a thesis. Take Columbus. He said the world must be round and set out to prove it."

"I'm not much of an adventurer," said David. "At least according to a certain someone."

"Aha! A certain someone. A certain girl, I'll wager. There's no dessert unless you come clean, my boy. What has this Aphrodite put you up to?"

Aphrodite? Did he mean the Goddess of Love? Meaning he was under some kind of spell? It spooked him to think that anyone could see through him so quickly. David shrugged and turned his attention to the meal, amazed at the three courses Alex had laid before them — trout, lamb curry accompanied by a smorgasbord of condiments like coconut, banana, jalapeno pepper and yoghurt, and finally fruit and cheese. Old Alex, the whites of his eyes brown with age, served without a murmur, never lingering, as if he were attending on royalty.

"How'd you get those scars?" The question slipped out.

Ngoma lowered his fork stuck with a plump chunk of tender lamb and looked at the back of his hand.

"*Duma*," he said with a hint of reticence in his voice.

"A what?" said David, putting his fork down.

"Cheetah," he said. He resumed eating. "The bugger wouldn't let go."

"He must have," David said.

"Only after my auntie massaged his throat and whispered in his ear." The highway minister's eyes deepened with memories flooding back.

"You couldn't do that to a grizzly," said David.

37

"A what?"

"A grizzly bear. Where I come from you'd need to sweet-talk a grizzly. But they don't listen so good."

"No, I suppose not," said Ngoma. "But a duma is something special. You see, it can almost be tamed from the wild."

"Almost," said David.

"Auntie thought she had won the heart of the chap. But what do we know of the heart? Mmmm?"

"Not much," said David.

"Of the untamed heart we know less. Except that it is powerful and it does not ask questions."

"I know. It jumps. Without even looking."

"You know this for a fact, do you?" said Ngoma.

"I'm working on it," said David.

"Yes, so am I. Well, I am glad to hear Americans are pondering such things."

David started eating again. He'd never been called an American before. He was Canadian and proud of it. On the other hand, he was a fugitive in a foreign land and feeling less sure of himself every hour.

"I was only seven," volunteered Ngoma. "My cousin, he was twelve."

"The cheetah jumped him, too?" asked David.

Ngoma made a blade of his hand and slashed his leg. "Is he —?"

"Alive and well!" said Ngoma, biting into a flat *chapatti* bread. "The happiest man alive!" Ngoma laughed out of pride or envy or even sadness, David couldn't tell.

Alex hurried onto the patio and spoke to Mr. Ngoma of a phone call that brought the Highways Minister to his feet and into the house. Fatigue pre-empted David's curiosity. As he mopped up gravy with the last *chapatti*, he remembered another big cat he'd seen. Less than a week ago. In MacGregor's house. A leopard. Stuffed.

David had visited Mr. MacGregor with the purpose of eating a little crow. Along with everyone else, he had wanted that classic '53 Mercury. He had found his teacher at home in his floor-to-ceiling book-jammed library, high on a stepladder dusting a stone bust of Zeus among other artefacts from a lifetime of travel and adventure. MacGregor wore loafers, dockers, and a tan fishing vest over a hairy chest. Without even a hello he'd told David he had been thinking about the Hanging Gardens of Babylon. David had told him he should write a book. The comment had been only partly facetious and MacGregor, as usual, heard what he wanted to hear.

"Excellent idea, Livingstone. The Wonders of the World contain the seeds of dreams — and don't we all need those?"

"I've been dreaming, sir. Of your car, actually." He'd placed a steadying hand on the ladder because five steps up MacGregor gazed into space, still talking of dreams, even if he seemed to be speaking to himself.

"You only need close your eyes and you're there."

"Where would that be?" asked David.

"Ah! That depends," said MacGregor. "The mighty Zambezi River perhaps. Standing at the brink of the mile-wide chasm into which it plunges and out of which rises a swirling mist like smoke from Hell." He'd squeezed the trigger on his spray bottle, sending a mist descending over David.

"You've been there, sir?"

SMOKE THAT THUNDERS

"Imagine, Livingstone, a river charged with a million gallons a second. Can you imagine the power? I have to tell you — on the q.t. — it's better than sex."

MacGregor hadn't asked David to verify his opinion. Instead, he'd continued speaking of this famous river flowing as smooth and heavy as glass right up to the crest, then surrendering its dark and silent river-nature without complaining. He'd compared it to giving up his own ego, his own personal history, and had thanked the gods for intervening in his fate, for leading him to darkest Africa so that he could acquire a taste for becoming one with the most awesome forces of nature.

"Fate?" said David. "I hate the idea of being controlled by someone else."

MacGregor had started down the ladder. "Of course. It's only a philosophic construct. And if you're not a philosopher or a poet you'll probably just imagine the thrill of jumping over the edge."

"I confess, sir, that's me." David only now noticed that Mrs. MacGregor had entered the library carrying a tea tray. "I think of jumping all the time," David said.

"Then you're just what a woman seeks in a man." She had an English accent and a firm voice, yet the glint in her eye warned against taking her too seriously. "Actions speak clearly while philosophy so often beats about the bush." She had moved through French doors onto the patio and had set the tray on a low glass table supported by a stuffed leopard. The cat was crouched, ready to attack.

"Time to change the subject, Livingstone," said MacGregor. "Anne believes that the good doctor should have named the falls after his long-suffering wife, Mary, and not after some old gal who, as fate would have it, happened to be Queen."

"And upon whose illegal empire the sun never set," she'd added before turning to her husband and pouring his tea. "My James would have named the falls after me, wouldn't you have, dear?"

"My dear, without you I wouldn't have cared if there were such things as Wonders of the World, much less have gone there." He'd winked at David and pointed him into a chair. "In those days I wouldn't even have got out of bed."

Anne had sighed. "We didn't get out of bed much, did we dear?"

"So, anyway," David had said, "how many miles does she have on her?"

Mr. MacGregor had looked confused.

"The Mercury, sir."

"The car, dear, the car," Anne had said. "You promised me you'd get rid of it."

"Stop! Stop, I say!"

David woke, startled, lost to time and place.

"You bastards!" Ngoma's shouts came from somewhere outside.

David found himself under a blanket on a cot in a screened-in porch. He'd slept through the night with his clothes on.

He tracked Ngoma to the front courtyard where he and Alex concerned themselves with a black three-ton truck parked on the highway at the bottom of the long driveway. Ngoma marched to his Mercedes, opened the door, turned on his in-car two-way radio and called "Charlie Victor Romeo". Alex, who had that towel draped over his forearm again, ran farther down the driveway shouting in Swahili.

One of the truckers, a gaunt Tanzanian wearing greasy overalls and a red bandanna on his head, restrained a child while his partner, a massive Sikh with a black turban, pried the boy's fingers from a bicycle wheel and tossed it onto stacks of other tires in the truck's metal cage. The leaner brute pushed the kid into the ditch and climbed aboard the battered truck, finessing it into first gear.

David ran as far as the gate and saw the boy vanish into the trees, crying. He picked up a rock and braced himself to throw it at the driver whom he could see more clearly now. A copper ring hung from one earlobe and a patchy beard grew around his mouth, lending the impression he'd just bitten the rear end out of a warthog.

"Come away," Alex said.

David watched the truck build a head of steam, then hurled the stone before it moved out of reach. The rock dropped through the open mesh of the cage behind the cab, smashing glass.

The truck stopped and reversed hard through its own exhaust to the foot of Mr. Ngoma's drive. The huge, black-bearded one stood on the running board with a five-foot length of rubber hose that he twisted menacingly in his fat hands.

Alex put a hand on David's shoulder and coaxed him toward the house.

"Pick on someone your own size, assholes!" David yelled.

The Sikh jumped to the ground and waddled toward the gate like a sumo wrestler, then, like a peasant nearing the threshold of the landlord's door, he stopped short. His shirt, long ago white and huge as a tent, had one sleeve ripped off at the shoulder exposing biceps as thick as a Christmas turkey. He bit on the hose out of frustration, or as a dire warning, it was hard to tell, then returned to the truck while his partner growled up a curse in Swahili along with phlegm that he spat in David's direction. The truck lurched forward belching sickeningly sweet diesel fumes, leaving David with a taste in his mouth he would not soon forget.

"I'll take care of those pirates," said Ngoma. He was still speaking to Charlie Victor Romeo on the car radio. "They won't get far. Carry on, Charlie Victor Romeo. I'll give you a shout if I need you."

David shook Alex's hand goodbye, thanked him for dinner last night and got in the passenger side. Ngoma signed off and hung up the mike.

"There you are, Livingstone. Thank God. I thought you'd died."

"I'm ready when you are," said David.

"Well, I'm not ready until I've had my tea, young man."

Before either of them were out of the car, Alex had placed a tray holding an ornate silver tea set on the hood of the Mercedes. Ngoma stirred three lumps of sugar into his steaming cup and drank it in one draft, like a potion. He took his suit jacket from Alex, put it on and presented himself to his servant for what must have been their ritual inspection. Alex slapped his palms together, held them in prayer mode and bowed.

"Let's go," said Mr. Ngoma. "For the sake of *Ujamaa!*"

FIVE

David had pictured Africa as the lush homeland of gorillas and crocodiles. The terrain he and Mr. Ngoma travelled through, however, was home to bleached grasses growing in red and dusty soil. Ngoma pointed out the baobabs, the elephants of trees that stood alone like grey monoliths, their gnarled, bare branches grappling for the sky. The devil, Ngoma said, uprooted the baobab and set it on its head. Trees called pau paus sprouted pendulous fruit like giant testicles that hung from pubic tufts high on spindly trunks. All of these wonders grew on a plain of spiky sisal gone to seed. When the rope industry switched to nylon, explained Ngoma, no one wanted sisal any longer and Tanzania lost a valuable export.

They sped along roads cluttered with cows and people whose movements lacked the road-wise flow of city traffic. Cyclists straining under enormous sacks of charcoal wavered and wobbled within a spoke of death, and women balancing bundles half again as large as themselves led children-in-tow to one side. Criss-cross cows took only as many steps as necessary to let the Highways Minister through.

David loved the anthills. Like rockets, old and rusted, they dominated lumpy stumpy fields where women, wrapped in red, yellow and green *khangas* stirred up cocoons of dust, digging with simple hoes. A man crouched in the open to take a dump. David wondered how he would wipe himself. Any supple leaf would do, he'd imagined, but here in the interior it was the end of the dry season. Next to the horror of having crap caked to his ass, it was the burnt-out hulks of cars and trucks that obsessed him. They littered the road, one per mile, almost without fail.

"What's *Ujamaa?*" said David.

"Brotherhood," said Ngoma. "Familyhood, to be more precise." Ngoma pulled hard at the wheel to avoid a pothole in a road that had once been paved but was now so eroded and broken it resembled a crumbling strip of burnt bacon. "It saddens me to think what my people do to each other."

As Ngoma cut the corner on a sharp bend, David saw a group of men and women ahead cannibalizing an abandoned Peugeot by the side of the road. Ngoma braked but didn't come to a stop until he'd passed them by thirty yards.

"It pains me, Sir David," said Ngoma, his voice rising in anger, "how difficult it is to live in harmony. For want of brotherhood we have socialist governments like ours who must take responsibility!" He slammed his hand on the steering wheel, then reached under the driver's seat for a socket wrench and got out. The scavengers around the Peugeot scattered like jackals in deference to the lion. David followed Ngoma to the wreck.

"Who to blame for roads rife with drunks and bandits? Who?" Ngoma demanded. "Who to blame if our precious goods cannot travel freely along this great international highway? Who? Who?"

"Ngoma," said David.

"Yes! Ngoma! That's who!" Ngoma removed his suit jacket and handed it to David before leaning into the Peugeot engine to unscrew a spark plug. "Ngoma, who was born a simple man," he continued, "Ngoma, who never forgets his roots in a poor village. Where, when he was just a scrap of a boy, he met the fateful duma. Damn!"

Ngoma retreated from the engine cursing grease on his cuff, and passed the wrench to David. "You have a go," he said, wiping his hands.

The duma again, thought David. He felt his pulse quicken at the mention of that animal. He unscrewed the first of eight spark plugs and handed it to Ngoma who stood by the fender.

"It was a monthly pilgrimage — my auntie, my cousin and I, along the river trail to Grandmother's house." Ngoma spoke in long, strong, whispered words in the manner of a child's tall tale. "We would bring her a bag of mealie meal and she in turn would fill us with praise we didn't deserve and bless us with stories of her youth."

"Then along came the big bad wolf," said David. Ngoma looked at him blankly.

"Sorry," David said.

"Auntie sensed the cat following us and stopped," Ngoma continued. "We snacked on dried fish at the river's edge. I soon saw that her ploy was to tease him with a morsel she left on a log, and so I did the same. We had not gone thirty feet when the cheetah claimed it without breaking stride."

Ngoma stopped at the sound of a distant rumble and put on his jacket. David emerged from the engine.

"Without warning he took my hand in his mouth," Ngoma continued.

"The fishiness," said David. "On your hand. He bit the hand that fed him."

"Exactly!" Ngoma looked back along the road in the direction of the rising thunder. "Come!"

Ngoma ran for the Mercedes and fired it up. David followed him and stood by the car door, curious about the roar. Ngoma didn't wait for him to get in. He drove ahead off the road and into the ditch leaving David to catch up on the run. Before David could take cover, the crescendo hit with the momentum of a locomotive. He braced himself against the car and made out the form of a passing petrol tanker through the gale of dust. When he could no longer breathe, he jumped in the Mercedes and watched in awe as, one after another, a convoy of tankers eighteen-strong passed in a dusty whiteout. As they waited for the dust to clear, Ngoma shut the engine off and continued his story.

"Auntie told me not to move. She stepped towards me but the cheetah grumbled from his gut. I could feel it, David. For a few moments I lived as though I were inside the belly of that beast."

Ngoma stared straight ahead as if the story emanated from the pit of the engine. David opened the window a crack to release the heat of the drama. Ngoma started up the engine but, before he put it in gear, a motorcycle passed at high speed. The rider acknowledged them with a gentle wave of the hand, like the Pope. When Ngoma crossed himself, David did a double-take on the rider. Black-robed, leather-helmeted and begoggled, he didn't look like any holy man David had ever seen.

"So, what happened next?" said David.

They were on the road again, driving through a thin veil of dust that refused to settle. Ngoma didn't answer and David didn't push. He was sure Mr. Ngoma would volunteer more on his own, and he might have, had they not rounded a curve to find one of the petrol tankers on its side blocking the road, it's payload leaking in a slow but steady stream into the ditch. It must have been the caboose of the convoy because the only one roadblocked was the priest. While he tried to rescue the driver from the smoking cab, villagers arrived armed with buckets to scoop up free fuel. On top of all that, literally on top, were the truckers David had seen earlier, the two thugs who had stolen the boy's wheel. They perched like vultures atop the tanker and unbolted the wheels.

Ngoma brought the Mercedes to a halt at a safe distance and got out. He warned everyone to move away. The petrol needed only one spark to send everyone to kingdom come. Ignoring his own advice, he took off his suit coat again and marched toward the truckers.

He knew them, or at least he knew of them — Albert and Sadarji. Sadarji, the man-mountain, lifted a tire off its lugs, threw it over the tanker out of sight and followed Albert off the rig as fast as his bulk would allow.

Mr. Ngoma cursed them in that booming voice of his. He also cursed government regulations stipulating that in situations like this the injured party gets first priority. After ordering David to record the thieves' licence number, he helped Father Manon — it seemed he knew everybody — pull the driver from the wreck.

Rounding the tanker, David found the thieves already aboard their black truck with engine revving and gears grinding. He stole close to the tailgate and found the licence plate caked with mud. He jabbed his elbow against the mud pack and it fell away, but before he could commit the number to memory, the truck lurched backwards, knocking him down. Sadarji got out and peered under the chassis.

"Where is he?" he growled. He had legs like tree trunks and boots as big as car batteries. The truck pulled ahead. "Where is he?!" Sadarji stomped his feet like a half-blind rhinoceros. He couldn't see David watching from behind the grill of the overturned tanker, nursing a scraped hip.

"God, he is everywhere, *mon petit*," said Father Manon who appeared unexpectedly.

From where David lay he could study this pointy-nosed Manon with his thigh-length frock, shin-high riding boots, and grimy hair that protruded from under his helmet. He held his ground as Sadarji lumbered toward him, the earth shaking as he walked, clouds of dust rising from each footfall.

"He was here!" said Sadarji.

"What do you mean, was?" said Manon. "God, He is the present tense. He is everywhere, and I am his servant come to tell you what's up."

This priest had such a strange and aggressive way of talking that David couldn't figure out if he was pious or not, but he had the moves down — he extended his hand for Sadarji to kiss. "I am the gate, *toé mon gros plein de merde!*" said Father Manon.

"If I find your gate in my way once more — " Sadarji stalled in the face of Manon's outstretched hand.

"Watch it, Big Guy," said Manon. "You never gonna get inside the Kingdom of God with a big mouth like dat."

"I rip you from your hinges!" said Sadarji much less sure of himself. He was mesmerized, it seemed to David, by the Holy man's ruby ring, and he backed off and climbed aboard the truck which moved away, backfiring.

"You speak like the little child who must come on hands and knees before you ever gonna get inside the Kingdom of God. Trust me, big guy."

David found villagers comforting the injured tanker driver in the back seat of the Mercedes while Mr. Ngoma stood outside the car talking into his radio microphone. He advised Dodoma Hospital of his estimated time of arrival and confirmed that, yes, it was "the same old thing". Over and out. Ngoma switched his mike to public announcement mode and told everyone to clear out because the petrol could explode any minute.

"So, you see, Sir David, what beastly obligation falls upon one too damned full of the milk of human kindness." Ngoma turned to the villagers to prove the point. "Who is your most obedient servant?" he demanded.

"Ngoma, that's who!" they said as one voice.

"Ngoma, who was once a free man like all of you!" he shouted as he settled in behind the wheel.

David hung by the window as Ngoma fired up the engine.

"Now you know, David, why we call it the Hell Run."

"What do I do now?"

"Come with me if you wish. But your goal is westward to the centre of the continent." Ngoma put the car in gear.

"Where am I?"

"Suffice to say you're on the only road there is to the place you are going. I wish you God's speed."

David followed Ngoma as the car started to move forward. In a matter of hours he'd become attached to Ngoma and his manner, his way of speaking and his stories. He couldn't let go.

"How did you get away?" he asked. "Did your aunt really whisper in the cheetah's ear?"

"Yes, she did."

"What about your cousin?"

"Young man, you have many questions. If I'm not careful you will discover how little I know about some things."

"What do you mean?" David had to trot to keep up.

"The duma had me by the hand, to be sure," said Ngoma. "And he wanted the fish, yes. But, officially, he had come for Auntie."

"He got her too?"

"Yes and no."

"What do you mean?"

"That's all I can say, I'm sorry!" Ngoma had to yell because he was leaving David behind. "Yes and no! I'm afraid it's the only answer I have to life's most important questions!"

The momentum of David's curiosity kept him running after the Mercedes even as it pulled away. Finally, he stopped and watched Ngoma disappear.

"*Allons-y!*"

David turned around and saw Father Manon sitting on his black and red Kawasaki, gas cap in hand, while a village elder filled his tank from a bucket.

"Can I come with you?" yelled David.

"I said, let's go! I invite you on a journey through God's country." Manon kick-started those six hundred and fifty cubic centimetres into a metallic racket that brought David running.

With one foot on the passenger stirrup, David noticed locals preparing to strip the tanker to the bare bones. Two men were already dismantling the radio while others were under the hood like surgeons performing an autopsy, nobody speaking, as if out of respect for the deceased.

"Shouldn't you stop them?" said David.

"I have news for you, my son," said Father Manon. "God, he like those who help themselves. For you, He has made already, a miracle, *n'est-ce pas?*"

Manon was right. What else to call his escape from Vancouver? The universe opened its doors and he walked through. The miracle had demanded a radical change of character, however, and David likened himself to Dr. Jekyll and his struggle to contain the grotesque Mr. Hyde. Was this journey a sign of David's dark side acting out? If so, was he insane? And if so, he was doomed. What the hell kind of miracle was that?

David hopped onto the saddle behind Father Manon and hung on. In two beats of the heart, the Kawasaki leapt forward into the drainage ditch beside the road, splashed through a river of petrol, skirted the rear end of the fallen tanker, climbed the road bed and blasted along the Hell Run heading west.

SIX

On the seventh day, God, he kick back and say, 'Blessed are dey who come unto me.' So, I take one small step toward God. I make myself the priest!"

Manon had to lean back and crank his head ninety degrees to be heard. David didn't encourage it; he wanted both the Father's eyes on the road.

"And God, he take the giant step toward me. He provide for me everything!" Father Manon took a hand off the handlebars and slapped the gas tank.

David would have argued that holy men respond to God's calling, not the other way around. Still, he liked Manon's approach of putting ideas into God's head.

Folks recognized Father Manon and waved. In return, the priest blessed them all with a benign little dip of the hand. He blessed ugly-as-sin warthogs that hustled stiff-legged across the road in front of him. He blessed wild turkeys and dead snakes. He killed a tsetse fly that stung him on the back of the neck and he blessed it before flicking it into the wind. He blessed drivers coming the other way and, of course, he blessed God *en haut*, up there. And he blessed the tire thieves when he caught up with them and passed them, in spite of Albert's attempts to side-swipe him. David gave them the middle finger of his left hand. Father Manon blessed cows and kids and a corporal who tacked a poster to a tree in front of a crowded market. Manon blessed everything except chickens. There were far too many chickens, and it was a miracle that David and Manon didn't run into one.

David tapped Manon's helmet and asked him to pull over. He wanted to go back and examine that poster. The photo it featured looked disturbingly familiar.

Manon pulled off the road and stopped at a shabby little "bottle shop" that stood alone at a junction with a rough and dusty side road. Tinny Congolese music came from within a walled enclosure behind the store.

David eased off the motorcycle. Saddle vibrations had numbed his crotch. It was absurd, but he needed to verify the whereabouts of his penis. He began to unbuckle his jeans when the shop door opened and a man hurried out carrying a basin of water. Behind him scurried his brood of five children followed by their mother with a newborn. She dropped to one knee in front of Manon, took his hand and kissed it. David rushed toward the shop but got no farther than the door. It sported one of those posters, and it was him all right.

REWARD NOTICE
100,000 SHILLINGS
FOR INFORMATION LEADING TO THE CAPTURE OF
DAVID LIVINGSTONE
WANTED FOR:
FRAUD
ILLEGALLY ENTERING THE COUNTRY
ESCAPING POLICE CUSTODY

One thing saved David from panicking — his own reflection in the window of the door. He didn't recognize himself beneath the mask of red dirt.

Father Manon took off his gloves to freshen up in the bowl that the shopkeeper had set upon the Kawasaki saddle. On the priest's command, the eldest son ran inside for two Cokes.

Ablutions complete, Manon sucked on his Coke bottle, then received the baby, holding it up like a human sacrifice. The other children, aged two to ten, crowded around him. They were a ragged little troupe except for new Bata sneakers they all wore on their feet.

"Do you believe?" Manon shouted.

"What?" David turned, caught red-handed removing the poster from the door. But Manon wasn't talking to him and so nobody noticed.

"Aye, Father. My son is a believer," said the mother, tears flooding her eyes. Manon dipped his finger in the dirty water and, with it, anointed the baby on the forehead and, in turn, the eyes, the ears and the chest.

"And does your little *chouchou* believe in Jesus Christ, born of the Holy Smoke and the Virgin Mary? Who was crucified but who never say die and who wind up on the right hand of God and who is gonna judge what the heck we do when the push come to shove?"

"Aye, Father," answered the woman.

David moved in behind the family to see if what he thought was happening was really happening.

"And does he believe in the Holy Spirit?"

"Aye, Father."

"And is he gonna forgive the International Monetary Fund when this country go on the auction block?"

"Aye, Father."

"Then I baptize you, little guy," said Manon as he performed the sign of the cross over the innocent child. "I baptize you Jean Beliveau Sadomba. In the name of the Father, Son and Holy Smoke. How do you like that?" Mom accepted her son back like the star he now was.

Manon winked at David. "And what about you, *mon fils?* Do you believe?" David turned at the sound of an approaching truck.

"I believe we better get outa here, Father," he said. Manon must have believed the same thing because he bolted for the bottle shop.

Inside, they watched at the window to confirm their fears. At the first sign of the tire truck stopping, the proprietor installed David amongst flats of empty Coke bottles under the counter and directed Father Manon through a rear door to join the sounds of partying and the vile smell of sour beer. David couldn't see out the window but he could hear the tell-tale clatter of the tire truck coming to a halt. He could hear the cage door open and the sound of a Kawasaki being tossed in and he wondered why, with criminals like these on the loose, *his* face adorned all these wanted posters? His relative innocence was a moot point, however, as Albert and Sadarji entered the shop and pushed through to what sounded like good times out back. David knew he should have split but his curiosity got the better of him. He eased open the door to the bar.

Fifty or sixty people were drinking in a brick-walled yard behind the bottle shop. Patrons sat on benches drinking bottled beer or homebrew from plastic lard buckets. Loud music made it difficult to talk, so that those who wanted to chat bunched together and yelled, while those who danced, danced close. Albert and Sadarji weren't talking or dancing; they had eyes for Manon and they found him holding court in the far corner.

Three heavy women and an effeminate old man in a cape made from a white sack and brown chicken feathers had gathered at Manon's feet to listen to his rant. As Sadarji and Albert pushed the women aside to position themselves in front of the priest, the music stopped. David caught the tail end of Manon's sermon which, now that silence prevailed, he aimed at everyone within earshot. According to Manon, the Book of Hebrews recommended "harbouring strangers". By accident you just might "entertain angels unawares". Sadarji glared at him.

"Take a number," said Manon.

David couldn't figure out why Albert and Sadarji would stoop on one knee before Manon. With these heathens so submissive before him, what could the good Father do but hold out his hand for respectful kisses? Sadarji took the holy hand, all right. He twisted the ruby ring off the finger and held it up to the light. Then he spat on it, tossed it to the ground and wiped his spittle-soaked hand on Manon's sleeve. Manon stood up, as indignant as Jesus in the temple of the moneylenders, and pointed to the exit.

"*Va t'en! Colis!*" His shortened cassock billowed with a fury that seemed to buoy him up, even off the ground. He might have walked on water, he looked that righteous. But since Albert had buckled Manon's boots together he went nowhere but forward over Sadarji's shoulder. The Sikh stood up and paraded him around like a sack of mealie meal.

Name-calling escalated into pushing and shoving between those for and against Father Manon. Someone hurled a bucket of home-brew beer at Albert. The acrid brew unfurled over the patrons like a sheet of vomit. David turned his back on shouts and breaking glass and hurried from the shop.

Outside, in the tire truck's cage, two boys lifted a heavy tire off the flatbed to liberate a bicycle wheel. What goes around, comes around, thought David. He joined the boys in the cage and wrestled Manon's Kawasaki to the tailgate. The kids scattered when a jeering mob exploded out of the bottle shop, floating the thieves out of there like flotsam on a storm surge. David had no option but to retreat deep within the jumble of tires. He caught a glimpse of Albert's bald skull bleeding badly as his partner heaved him into the cab. David heard the crowd shriek and a boy scream. Through the tires he saw Sadarji holding a small boy to his face as if he might eat him like a samosa.

"Hey! Fat man!" David yelled. "I said, pick on someone your own size!"

Sadarji let the kid drop. A bottle hit him on the back of the turban but he didn't flinch. The kid kicked him in the shin and ran but Sadarji ignored it. He circled the truck and, as he rounded the tailgate, he slammed the bolt into the cage door latch, then waddled back to the cab and pulled himself up behind the wheel.

David was lying close enough to the back of the cab that he could hear Albert's groaning and Sadarji's laboured breathing. How long would it be before they found him? he thought. As the truck moved forward and continued up the Hell Run, Sadarji began singing a lullaby and soon Albert stopped moaning. Evening, then night, provided

David an extra blanket of protection as they drove, and he ceased worrying about being eaten alive.

Through a gap in the tires he saw a half moon rising into a band of cloud. Flickering lights from a steady stream of cooking fires spoke to him in code. Funny how darkness has a way of making you see, he thought, not what's out there but what's inside. The dot-dash-dot code spoke to that dark place where passion is blind, yet plows its way forward. The message decoded said, *Go, Davey, go!*

The journey to the interior proceeded without interruption. The rhythm of thumps and bumps wove a veil of sleep over David. The image of Errol Livingstone appeared — a close-cropped bearded man at the wheel of a solid steel, Mad Max all-terrain vehicle crossing the Sahara solo in a sand storm, day sixteen in the gruelling twenty-two-day Paris-to-Dakar Rally that would end on the west coast of Africa for those lucky enough to make it and would cost the lives of a few who didn't. A phone was ringing. David could see his father reaching for a car phone and for a second felt like he might get the chance to speak with him — until the phantom four-by-four vanished from sight behind a curtain of blowing grit and David awoke, shivering with cold. The tire truck had stopped. It was still night.

"Get the phone! I am busy!"

The voice didn't belong to either Albert or Sadarji but to someone more officious. David could see a light. Shifting his position, he saw that it issued from a metal hut where a soldier stood talking on the phone. David could make out a voice over the rumble of the truck's idling engine.

"What is the charge? Escaping custody? Very serious. You can count on Sergeant Bukoba."

The phone receiver banged down. Someone loaded shells into a rifle. Feet crunched over gravel, getting closer, until David caught a glimpse of this soldier named Bukoba circling the cage inspecting the cargo. He wasn't as large as a man with a name like Bukoba should be. He had a big voice but a small head. The sleeves of his camouflage shirt were rolled up to the thickest section of his biceps which weren't very thick at all. The peak of his cloth cap obscured his eyes in shadow.

"Opening up! Now!" The sergeant in command eyed the Kawasaki. "Bring the Sikh!" Another soldier ushered Sadarji to the tailgate. "Such things are not permitted for export," said the sergeant named Bukoba.

Export. This must be the Zambian border, David thought.

"Goodness, such low retail value, I assure you," said Sadarji.

"Not permitted! Open, please!"

From where David lay among the tires, he could hear Sadarji undo the catch and struggle against gravity to mount the flatbed. Once the Sikh was in the cage, David saw him pick up the Kawasaki, but slowly, in order to observe through the broken back window of the cab how Albert slipped into the driver's seat. Sadarji held on to the cage as Albert gave it gas. Too much gas. The motorcycle and a dozen tires slid out of the cage onto the road. The truck rammed the border gate but didn't have enough momentum to break through. It reversed into a U-turn and returned full throttle, forcing the soldiers to jump aside. David leapt from the truck's tailgate and scrambled on hands and knees to the opposite side of the road. He heard shouts and gunshots and the careening of bullets off metal as he grovelled through a ditch on his belly towards the trees without once looking back.

He ran through woods until he met a six-foot-high coil of barbed wire. Bullets threaded the metal web, making it sing like a swarm of robotic insects. He ran parallel to the border wire hoping for a break. Barbs tore his arm so he angled away and ran through the darkness until the sound of gunfire grew faint. He ran until he ran without fear but even then he didn't stop. He didn't stop until he reached the shore of a small river where he crouched down in soft grasses to catch his breath.

David lowered himself into the water to rinse blood off the gash on his arm. He waded deeper even though the cuts stung and moonlight threatened to give him away. He stayed there until he heard a low growl from the far bank. As he retreated to the shore he saw a thatched hut by the water's edge fifty yards downstream. With no sign of anyone about he walked the river trail to the low hut, peered into the gloom and saw a blue wooden rowboat. He ducked down to enter the doorway and curled up in the boat, but couldn't stop shivering.

SEVEN

D avid woke but didn't move.

"Mzee! Have you seen a *mzungu?*"

"A *mzungu?* Nay, Angel Bukoba."

This "Angel" sounded like the sergeant from the border post. The other voice was older, gentler and very close by.

"Old man, you are speaking to Sergeant Bukoba! These are stripes, can't you see? One, two, three. Now tell me, where is this *mzungu?* He is in big trouble, like yourself!"

"Changwe makes no trouble," said the older man.

"I will be there when you tell such lies to the judge," yelled Sergeant Bukoba.

David lifted his head and peered over the gunwale. A canoe on the river drifted out of sight behind the low door frame of the boathouse.

"But good luck to you, Mzee," the sergeant added, as a kind afterthought, it seemed to David.

Minutes passed. Nothing moved except the river past the boathouse door. David ached all over. Since the man who called himself "Changwe" had last spoken, there had been no sound of his moving either closer or farther away. The gurgling of the river reminded David of falling asleep last night when he had felt finally free, far from trouble, far from highways and highwaymen, far from everything. For all he knew, he might have slept around the clock. Then, he heard a tapping.

"I see you are wearing shoes from America." The voice was Changwe's.

David crawled out far enough to see a one-legged man supporting himself on a crude crutch, the stump of his missing limb visible within the leg of his threadbare khaki shorts. He must have been fifty-five years old although his scrubbed complexion, smiling eyes and the glint off a silver-capped tooth suggested a younger spirit.

"I'm pretty much made in America," said David, figuring he would run with this deceit as long as he could.

"I am all for America," said old Changwe. "I am loving too much your President Nixon." He held out his hand.

David hesitated, reluctant to get involved with anyone new, especially under the pretences of posing as an American. Then he stood up and extended his hand to Changwe. The old man's hand was warm, tough, and relaxed. But what kind of time warp was he in? Nixon?

Mr. Changwe led David up the riverbank to a circle of round huts, four of mud and one of corrugated sheet metal, that sat on a rise of land above the river. Chickens foraged in the yard amongst furniture and appliances — an armchair, a fridge, a Sony Trinitron with funky push-button controls, a radio and a telephone — all in the open and unconnected to electricity and probably defunct but making an impression nevertheless.

Mr. Changwe was a sight now, too, standing in a pin-striped, double-breasted suit, even if it was too large and had one leg hanging empty. His daughter had been waiting for him to return so that she could pin it for alterations. "Too much bother, Pepsi," he said. "Too much fuss." This daughter whom Changwe called Pepsi must have been older than David by a year or two; or else it only seemed that way because she ignored him. What interested David most about Changwe's compound, however, was the Mercedes.

White with four doors like Mr. Ngoma's, this one had rusty scars across the roof that told the story of another Hell Run catastrophe. The car sat on logs with grass growing through the engine. Without doubt it had been the victim of vultures because it had no tires, which didn't surprise David at all.

"Does it run?" he asked.

Pepsi stood quietly at the cooking fire and poured boiling water into a teapot. Mr. Changwe was equally noncommittal as he eased himself into his armchair, taking care not to wrinkle the suit or let the pins prick.

"I'm talking about the car. If it started, do you think it would make it to Victoria Falls?" Pepsi stared at him, coldly.

"Sorry," David said, "I mean, Smoke That Thunders."

David had no trouble recognizing the silent treatment. He sat on the Mercedes' bumper and pulled hard on his boots. His wet feet had swollen overnight but he managed to remove one, which he threw to within a foot of Pepsi's cooking fire. Mr. Changwe broke the silence by telling David that Pepsi would soon be studying at the teacher training college in Dodoma, to which David nodded politely. He wondered why they hadn't bothered to ask his name.

"The name's Livingstone. David Livingstone." He hoped to get a rise out of someone, but no such luck.

Pepsi brought a loaded tea tray toward her father. Setting one end of the tray on a coffee table, she shifted a stack of magazines to make room for it.

"An innocent man should not try to be someone he is not," Changwe told her in a half whisper.

"Sometimes, better than claiming innocence is to respect the court," said Pepsi. "And anyway, Father, you are guilty. You took it. You drove it. It is against the law."

"Mr. Changwe, you stole a car?" said David.

"Don't you make it more difficult." Pepsi looked for the reprimand from her father, a facial gesture that told her she'd been impolite. She turned to David and said, "Please and thank you very much."

High on Pepsi's dominant cheekbones the skin was pockmarked but not enough to distract from her full-bodied beauty. She examined her father, apparently happy with the overall affect of his wardrobe except for his one bare foot.

David saw both of them glance at his boot lying by the fire.

"If I were you, I would not waste time in Tunduma village," she told David. "It is very far, this place you are going. A thousand miles, maybe more."

"That far?" asked David.

"Farther perhaps."

"In that case, I better get on my horse," he said.

"We are busy people, doing our duty to our country."

"Pepsi is quite right," said Changwe. "Every day it is my duty to measure the river."

"Not once but twice daily," said Pepsi, "now that the rains have come. "My father is a very important man."

"No problem. Sorry to bother you," said David. He retrieved the boot he'd removed and started to put it back on.

"A cup of tea takes no time," said Changwe.

With the boot stuck on his foot, David hopped to the bumper and sat down again. Pepsi set a teacup on the car fender.

"It is our custom to take tea from those who offer," she said.

David drank it like Ngoma, with one hand on his hip, in one go. Pepsi watched him, then handed him a plate of chocolate-covered digestive cookies and watched him eat three in a stack. He kicked off the boot and picked up a government-issue map from the table.

"It is said that my river reaches the Zambezi after many miles," said Mr. Changwe.

One boot on and one off, David took the map with him to the edge of the yard for a better view of the Kalungu river that wound its way south and west. The river turned a rocky bend and disappeared around a hillside covered with scarlet-leafed flamboyants and flat-topped thorn trees. He examined the map. Beyond the hill lay Zambia and somewhere off the map to the south flowed the legendary Zambezi. When he turned around, Changwe and his daughter were gone.

David took a closer look at the map. He pinpointed his location without a problem because the border between Tanzania and Zambia was on a neck of land between two great long lakes running north and south, Lakes Tanganyika and Malawi. For at least a thousand miles, only one route from the coast penetrated the interior, and this was it. From what David knew about the real Livingstone, he must have travelled close to this spot on his way north to Lake Tanganyika where Stanley caught up with him.

Mr. Changwe appeared from the equipment hut in his worn khakis, carrying a small wooden box with a brass handle, earphones, and notepad. Pepsi followed him out with the suit on a hanger. She placed sunglasses on her father's face and followed him down the hill toward the river.

Left alone, David picked up one of those magazines from the coffee table. They were American glossies from the seventies and eighties. He sat in Mr. Changwe's armchair and flipped through a back issue of *Time*. Way back, the year David was born. Washington State's Mount St. Helen's was blowing up on the cover.

Pepsi returned for a bundle of laundry, which she balanced on her head.

"You should not joke about that Livingstone fellow. Such a thing can get you into very big trouble." She proceeded toward the river trail once again.

"You're telling me!" David yanked off his other boot and followed her down.

Mr. Changwe sat in the blue boat, attending a line that fed over a pulley and into the water. The boat was attached to a cable that stretched across the river. Changwe kept an eye on his watch and made regular entries in his log book of sounds he must have been hearing through the earphones. When he saw David crouched by the boathouse with the map, he held up his earphones as an invitation for him to wade into the water and listen.

David stood in knee-deep water beside the boat and donned the headset. Electronic ticks from the revolving screw of a small submerged torpedo, Changwe explained, provided data for the calculation of the velocity and volume of the river. When David returned the earphones, Changwe pulled the boat three feet farther into the current and resumed counting.

From the cover of the boathouse, David could watch Pepsi wash clothes on a rock at the shore nearby, but mostly he studied the map for alternative routes to the Zambezi River.

"How often do you guys cut that tub loose?" he asked. Pepsi was close enough to hear but far enough away to pretend that she didn't.

"The boat is government property," she said after an awkward minute of silence. "It is not for pleasure."

David studied her as she squatted by the water's edge. Not only did she talk tough, everything about her seemed strong, even aggressive, but not outright hostile. She had triceps that Jackie would kill for.

David traced with his finger a series of watercourses flowing south, calculating the number of days the journey might take by river.

"Three days by boat to the Zambezi," he said.

"Why don't you swim? I have heard that American boys can do anything," she said.

David detected a smile trying to break out across her face. "You've been watching way too many movies," he said. "You have movies?"

"Of course," said Pepsi. "I have seen your Rambo. And it is my opinion that Americans should stay home."

"Hey, for your information," said David, "I'm Canadian, okay? And I agree, Americans should stay home."

Changwe lifted his head from his work. Pepsi waved to him, smiled, then turned, grim again, to David.

"Whatever you are, you have come at a bad time. My father needs no more trouble. It would be better if the duma takes his other leg than to have you riding about in a boat that is the property of the United Republic of Tanzania."

"Duma? You mean cheetah?" he asked.

Pepsi plunged a handful of soapy laundry into the stream.

"I heard a story about a couple of kids who were almost eaten by a duma," he said. He expected that to be the last word, and it was, but the look she gave him suggested that if he hung around long enough, more words would be forthcoming.

EIGHT

Their chores finished, Changwe and his daughter returned to their home on the rise without telling David to go or asking him to stay. He didn't know how to interpret that, so, he gave the Changwe's some breathing room and hiked downstream. The idea of proceeding by boat seemed, to David, the safest and most poetic way to go. MacGregor would approve, he thought.

A hundred yards downstream, the Kalungu picked up speed and became white and excited as it charged through an obstacle course of exposed bedrock. David followed it until it rounded a bend and became shallow and braided. The mud felt good oozing between his toes and he wondered why he couldn't walk the river, at least into Zambia. Visions of that fabled cheetah stopped him from trying it right now. That and the bridge.

As David approached the low, wooden span, the absence of traffic and a narrow road allowance suggested that this was no main road. Then he saw the telltale railway ties, and had started to climb the bank to investigate when he heard voices. He scurried for cover in the shadows at the foot of the wooden abutment. Something caught his eye

— his map in the water. It floated toward him from the direction he'd come. He felt his back pocket and discovered his passport gone, too.

The voices were on top of him by now. He looked up through the ties in the bridge deck and saw two soldiers aiming their rifles at someone on the other side — an old woman, bent and bowlegged under a load of firewood.

The soldiers interrogated her in Swahili. *Where are you going? Where have you come from?*; simple questions, David imagined, yet unreasonable demands in a free country. As the soldiers, who seemed hardly more than boys, crossed toward her, David pressed himself against the abutment and saw the map drifting beneath the bridge. The soldiers ordered the old lady to drop her load. They laughed and brandished their rifles about like playthings. One soldier noticed the map in the water on the other side of the bridge and fired at it.

Hundreds of tiny green birds, spooked out of nearby trees, flocked quickly and veered downriver. As the trigger-happy guards opened fire, David saw his passport floating toward him twenty yards upstream. He slipped into the water and submerged to his chin until the current delivered the passport into his hands. Once he grabbed it, he vanished beneath the surface of the river.

Upstream in reeds, he surfaced and immediately looked toward the bridge, sure of witnessing unspeakable atrocities being inflicted upon the poor old woman. Instead, he saw one of the soldiers leading the way across, carrying her bundle, while the other soldier led her graciously on his arm.

Above the rapids and around the rocky outcrop, David opened his passport. Jackie was as soaked as he was.

Texture had faded from her face rendering her cold as marble. She'd have plenty to say about his being trapped like a carp in this Tanzanian backwater, and it wouldn't be the first time she'd accused him of being "stuck".

They'd had long discussions about passion, or rather the lack of it. It was a malaise that infected the whole society, according to Jackie. Nobody wanted anything badly enough and she blamed television. She had donated her TV to an inner-city mission because, according to her, the business of Hollywood entailed hijacking dreams. We grow up not knowing what we really want or who the hell we are, she'd said. David recalled MacGregor saying in class that our dreams were the blueprints of the soul. Of course, Jackie had agreed immediately and whole-heartedly, as if her soul was the goddamn Taj Mahal. Which maybe it was. Certainly, in David's own mind he had built her up to be that perfect.

Back at the boathouse he laid Jackie on a rock. He was thinking she wouldn't take long to dry in the noonday sun when he heard the throaty roar of a motorcycle coming from the hilltop, from Changwe's yard. He heard, too, the sounds of chickens running for their lives. Under cover of bamboo, David crept to the edge of Changwe's circle of huts. Whoever caused the uproar was earning a piece of Pepsi's mind.

A soldier on a motorcycle rode herd on the chickens. The bike looked like Father Manon's and the soldier could have been the one at the border hut, the same sergeant who had warned Mr. Changwe about going to court, the one who called himself "Bukoba". If so, he was younger than David had imagined. His long neck and fine ears didn't correspond with the image of a fighting man.

Neither did his juvenile act of terrorizing chickens as he rode circles around Mr. Changwe who sat in his armchair oiling his brass torpedo. As Pepsi tried to catch an injured chicken that flopped about on one leg, the soldier turned off the engine and announced that a one-legged chicken should feel right at home here.

Mr. Changwe told Bukoba to act his age, which incited the sergeant to kick open the door to one of the huts. Pepsi vowed to report him to the judge. His jury of peers would remember him as a pathological liar, Pepsi yelled. They would drop the charge against her father and, instead, find him guilty of failing to live up to the name his poor mother gave him — "Angel Bukoba"!

Sergeant Angel Bukoba reappeared from the hut drinking from the same kind of plastic bucket that David had seen in the tavern behind the bottle shop. A chymous froth that looked in every way like puke hung from Bukoba's moustache. He paused to breathe and for his watery eyes to clear.

"And I will tell," Bukoba replied, "for what it is our hydro man takes a government salary!" Bukoba marched to the armchair, picked up Changwe's river gauging note-book and brandished it in his face, accusing him of taking pay for the work of a schoolboy. Pepsi snatched the book and reproached the sergeant for failing to understand science and for being ignorant of how engineers would use her father's data for agricultural and hydro-electric projects in the future. She brought the sergeant's entire education into question, doubting that "Angel Bukoba" could even spell his own name.

"Sergeant Bukoba! Have you not heard?" Bukoba pointed out his three stripes.

"We have heard that the village bully chases tourists through the *bundu*," said Pepsi.

Bukoba assured Pepsi that she would not be so rude when she was his wife. When Pepsi replied that she had every intention of respecting "her husband", whoever that might be, Bukoba braced to chuck the beer bucket at her but, instead, spit beer at a chicken.

"Such a fine boy you used to be," said Changwe.

Bukoba swaggered toward the Kawasaki and kick-started it. "Wind your watch, old man," he said. "The judge he is coming tomorrow. Do not be late." Then, as if he just remembered the purpose of his visit, he pulled one of those "Wanted" posters from his pocket, forced it on Mr. Changwe, and accelerated away.

Once he was out of sight, Pepsi took the poster from her father's hand and examined it.

"They say a man with one leg is not permitted to drive," said Changwe. "While drunkards like he — !" He ran out of words.

"While drunks like him rule the road," said David, emerging from the trees. "I know, this country's got worse drivers than back home."

Pepsi shut him up with a furious stare.

Later, as Pepsi cut her father's hair, David crouched by the cooking fire and studied alternative routes over the border. He held a rolled-up *People* magazine in his hand like a baseball bat. Every time he caught Pepsi watching him, he checked his watch as if he had a plane to catch.

This was supposed to be a hit-and-run operation, see Victoria Falls, buy a postcard, go home. Boiled down to its *TV Guide* essentials, it sounded pointless and David dreaded the thought of having to explain it. He'd side-stepped the issue with Mr. Ngoma, Changwe would probably never ask, but Pepsi? She made David nervous. She didn't play by the rules, didn't hesitate to speak her mind, which made him now realize he didn't know this escapade from one of Jackie's Harlequin Romances. Without a payoff, without a trophy of some kind, this trip wouldn't even amount to that.

"What if I cross the river and bushwhack to the highway a mile or so down the road?" He stood up and started pacing.

"We will pray that you are far away when the *mamba* bites you," said Pepsi as she brushed hair off her father's shoulders.

David uttered something under his breath, something about not being sure he could get far enough away. He watched Pepsi gather her comb and scissors and remind her father it was past his bedtime.

"There is a saying," Changwe said to David, "about a man who is bitten by the snake. If he can see his village, if he is that close, he will die."

"Why? What if he's way the hell out there?"

"He will not run home, he will keep his heart quiet," said Changwe. "He will think, he will do the right thing. He will rip his shirt, tie around his leg, and suck out the poison. "

"He will die a little more slowly," said Pepsi.

David watched her retreat to her hut, away from the firelight, so that her dark skin melted into the night, leaving her long back, narrow waist and powerful hips defined by the yellow of her cotton dress. He saw Mr. Changwe watching him, so he stood up and looked under the hood of the car.

"How do we know this baby won't fire right up?" David asked.

"In America, are they letting one such as me to drive the auto?" Changwe asked.

"Why not? You could take the test," said David.

"It is difficult?"

"Parallel parking. On a hill. That's the killer. But with a little luck, sure."

"I would very much like to visit America."

"You pretty much got it all right here," David said. He picked up the phone and actually listened for a dial tone before putting it down. "America is overrated. Trust me." David turned back to the Mercedes and pulled the crankcase dipstick out of its sheath.

"I would like to drive you to your destination, Mr. David," said Changwe.

"To Victoria Falls?"

"It would be my very great pleasure."

"Thanks, anyway, Mr. Changwe." David found only a trace of oil at the end of the dipstick. "And if I had wings, I'd fly us to the moon."

"Changwe dreams of a motor trip such as yours," he said, sitting forward in his chair. "Of seeing Mosi-O-Tunya rising in the sky."

"You've never been there?"

"Changwe wants to go. Many times he wants to go. Even practising to go! But —"

"Practising?

Mr. Changwe held an imaginary steering wheel in his hands.

"Practising on what?" David looked around. Changwe couldn't have meant the Mercedes. It hadn't been driven lately. "You mean the car you stole? That's why you stole it?" David howled with laughter, then sobered up. "So, you're serious."

"Aye, but it is very far, Mr. David."

"So what?"

"Nay, an old man such as I should forget such dreams."

David's heart went out to him. His heart went so far out it almost made him nauseous. An old man's dreams shouldn't be so far-fetched. He turned to the darkness under the hood of the car to conceal a sympathy that churned deep in his gut. He stared into the engine until, like a witch doctor consulting a dog's innards, he caught a glimpse of his own half-lived life, and it was not a pretty sight. He pulled two spark plugs from his pocket, the ones he'd scavenged from the Peugeot with Mr. Ngoma, and presented them to his new friend.

"Will these help?" said David. Changwe held them, one in each fist, like pistons.

"Changwe would drive until the lion in his heart cannot be heard for thunder. At Mosi-O-Tunya, I have heard there is too much thunder."

"That's what I've heard. A million gallons a second. That's what my teacher said," said David. He watched Changwe lean back into the armchair and close his eyes. On the old man's lap lay a *Time* magazine with Richard Nixon on the cover. David picked it up. April, 1974.

"Would you buy a used car from this man?" David asked.

"Surely!" said Changwe.

77

NINE

D avid slept like a wolf, waking every fifteen minutes. His dreams were short episodes, one after the other, full of desperation. At first light he awoke shivering. Curling up into his own warmth, he risked sleep again, and worse, another dream.

He was cycling alone in bare hills, working hard uphill, puffing and straining until the pain of trying became unbearable, then gliding down the lee side, giving himself up to the wind and the road and the black hills, his eyes closed, no hands, faster and faster, not daring to open his eyes, too late, feeling only speed and balance and the pressure of his own blood beating his heart, his knees pulled up, self-contained like a doomed astronaut awaiting the end.

He awoke suddenly to a yard that was quiet, except for the clucking of chickens. The warmth of the sun upon his feet in the doorway welcomed him back to earth. He looked around the shed at tools, tarps, gauge posts and paddles, and at a half-hidden Perelli Tires calendar, 1977. David took hold of an oar and, from where he lay, lifted the arm of a rain jacket to reveal a milk-white woman slipping out of something sheer. He shut the door with the oar to see another calendar in the corner. It featured a Porsche 917 winning the '73 Le Mans, but it disappeared from the winner's circle when the door opened unexpectedly and Pepsi entered with a cup of tea and left it for David without saying a word.

As the warm sweet tea relaxed his innards, he watched her move around the yard. She had that African way of bending from the waist to get low to sweep or to pick things up. He had always been told to bend the knees. He watched the way she walked, the way her ample rear swung, her whole body following after her pelvis. He could see something self-conscious in her eyes, a shyness that said, I don't mind you being here, even if everything else she did suggested otherwise.

After she left the yard, David continued to lie in his bed. With his foot he lifted a tarp to see what other treasures Changwe had hidden. "A battery!" He sat up and removed the tarp completely. Four good tires, on rims.

As he pulled on his boots, he remembered Changwe's cautionary words about "using his head and doing the right thing". After setting one tire on the Mercedes' right front lugs, David ran back to the shed for nuts. He found the tire iron with Changwe's other tools, but where were the lug nuts? He saw two of them in the corner. As he reached for them amongst mouse turds and dead flies, a shadow fell over him accompanied by the dull jingling of lug nuts in someone's hand. David's heart sank even before he turned and saw Sadarji filling the door frame.

He had never seen Sadarji this close up. Big like a Samoan, he had rope for suspenders. From between the

Sikh's wet lips came the acrid vapours of a recent meal, hot and sour, but he said nothing.

"Come back next week," said David. "We have all the tires we need." It didn't stand a chance of being funny.

"But we are always needing a few more," said Sadarji. He retreated, pulling the door shut, locking David in. Through the window, David saw Albert rolling a tire away. His red bandanna bulged over a bulky bandage on his skull. "Hey! Those tires belong to Mr. Changwe!"

"Yes, *mzee* has always such excellent tires," said Sadarji who appeared at the window. "The very best quality!"

"You bastards won't get away with this! Not this time, I promise you!" yelled David.

"But we do. Each and every time we are in Tunduma district!" said Sadarji as he rolled another tire to their truck.

David picked up a six-foot section of water level gauge post, smashed the window and climbed out. He rolled one of the two remaining tires to the trail that led to the river, gave it a well-aimed kick and followed it down.

Halfway across the river, Changwe was too absorbed in his submarine regime of tickings and calculations to notice the runaway tire. When it hit a rock by the shore, Pepsi turned from checking a fish net to see it balloon into the air. She had to dodge it before it splashed into the water, soaking her.

The tire sank before David caught up with it. As he hauled it out of the mud, Pepsi drew the photos of Jackie from her waistband like a pistol and brandished them in front of his face.

"Look what I have found by the river for all the world to see," she said. "Perhaps you would like to raise a flag with her pretty face upon it."

David reached for the photos but Pepsi withheld them. At the sounds of running, they turned to see Albert and Sadarji emerge from the bamboo trail. Pepsi splashed through shallow water toward them.

"You again! Thieves and cowards!" she yelled.

"Cowards? We are afraid of nothing," said Sadarji. He left it to Albert to catch David who continued to wrestle the tire out of the mud.

"You are animals! Like the duma that feeds only his stomach," shrieked Pepsi.

"Better than to starve like a civil servant!" roared Sadarji. He helped Albert hold David underwater until David relinquished his grip on the tire. Pepsi threw the net over Sadarji, enveloping him in the mesh and forcing him to release David.

"Pirates! So courageous you think you are! But I have news for you. It is only your belly that grows big on your courage!"

Albert slunk away with the tire as David spit up and gasped for air. Sadarji made his way to the shore like a bear in a tent, slashing at the netting with a nine inch blade, shedding it like an old skin and leaving it in shreds.

"Your heart is starving! Your soul, it is threadbare!" yelled Pepsi as she chased them up the path and out of sight.

Changwe abandoned his gauging and pulled the boat along the cable to shore. He fished the photos of Jackie from the water and handed them to David who remained knee-deep, trying to catch his breath.

"You must excuse my daughter," said Changwe.

David looked at the photos, then at Changwe, then up the path toward the compound where Pepsi could still be heard cursing the tire thieves.

"Never mind," David said. "You're not going to be too happy with me, either."

Changwe wrote off the loss of his tires with no more than a shrug. It seemed to matter more to him that David was here to transport him to the outside world via his personal stories. Back in Changwe's compound, they worked at close quarters under the hood of the Mercedes, installing the battery and filing the points on the distributor.

"These bank machines are cool. Your card goes in the slot, right? Then you punch in your ID number and the account you want to access."

David wore a frangipani *khanga* as a skirt. He wasn't trying to impress Mr. Changwe with all his high-tech culture as much as Changwe was drawing out of him everything he could about life in America.

"Then, however much you want to withdraw — fifty, a hundred, whatever — you just punch it in," said David.

"He does not understand what you are saying," said Pepsi from across the yard. She was repairing the fish net and it would take her the rest of the evening and the best part of some other day.

David walked across the yard toward Pepsi where his T-shirt and jeans hung on a clothesline strung between two huts. He pulled the VISA card from the trousers pocket.

"Don't leave home without it," he said. He didn't expect Pepsi to understand but he returned to the Mercedes and handed Changwe the credit card.

"Such a thing will not come to Tunduma village for a long time," said Changwe. He felt the plastic for stiffness, tapped it for hardness, and ran his finger tip over the embossed name and number. Then he moved his head left and right to sneak a peek at the little hologram of the bird taking flight.

"They've got cash machines everywhere," said David. "On the streets, grocery stores, airports."

"Is it true that a common man like me can purchase petrol far from home with such a thing?"

David leaned into Changwe's ear. "Even tires."

"Is everyone having such a thing?" said Changwe. He showed the card to Pepsi who watched curiously.

"Just about. And if not, hey!, borrow your mom's," said David. "Just kidding."

Pepsi left her fish nets and took dead aim on David. "In a civilized country such as ours you can go to jail for taking what is not yours."

She unfolded a Wanted Poster and thrust it at him — the latest edition. Since they'd upped the bounty to a million *shilingi*, it was creating all the excitement of a Presidential election, she said. According to her, Sergeant Bukoba had forced the poster upon villagers in the market and upon drivers at the Shell petrol pumps and bus passengers waiting at the Zambian border. And after he was sure no person would be able to close their eyes at night without David's face staring at them from the depths of their national duty, Bukoba apparently threw the remaining posters off a bridge so that they would float down the river to inform the hippos and the herons and the hartebeest.

David sat on the bumper and feigned indifference. Pepsi snatched the poster out of his hand and strutted back to her nets, saying she would not be surprised if Sadarji and Albert were the first to find one of these posters and were the first to come looking for him.

"It wasn't even my idea to come here, if you want to know the truth." David spit it out like venom. Pepsi turned on him.

"Fine. And now it is everybody's idea that you should go," she said, matching him spit for spat.

Changwe tried to mediate with subtle looks, one meant to cool Pepsi's jets and the other to beg David's forgiveness for her continuing rudeness. David barely noticed because, privately, he was retracting his too-quick retort that implied he wasn't here by choice. He was. He had gone to the airport to see his mother off, that much was true. When Jackie showed up, however, all lovey-dovey with her photos, he'd realized that his crisis didn't concern her. She had apologized and had said she loved him but it wasn't enough. He'd begun to burn inside because he didn't know why this love of hers, which was all he'd wanted, was not enough. He'd turned away from her because one of her looks might have quenched that fire. Had he been insane with fever? It was devouring him. He knew that there would be nothing left. Fine, he'd thought. Take me.

Mr. Changwe ran his finger around the edges of the credit card as if to conjure up the thrill of money for nothing.

"I would buy shoes," he said.

David set one of his cowboy boots beside Changwe's tough old foot. "I'll get you a pair. Two rights. It's a promise."

Changwe picked the boot up, looked it over and under and inside, then held it on his lap.

"Now, tell me please about your President Nixon," Changwe said.

Surely, they must know, David thought. "He's dead," he said.

Pepsi looked at him as if he'd just killed Nixon himself, then quit working and entered her hut. Changwe, too, retreated behind closed eyes. David went back to the Mercedes to see what he could do in what light remained. By the time he'd finished draining the oil from the crank case and straining it through a piece of cloth, Mr. Changwe was asleep in his chair, protected from the chill night air by a blanket Pepsi had laid over him.

David reintroduced the oil to the engine, then withdrew the dipstick and brought it into the light of Pepsi's paraffin lantern outside her hut where she was pressing clothes with a crude iron filled with glowing embers. He looked for the oil-level on the dipstick, felt the consistency of the oil and shook his head.

"A Mercedes should have Quaker State," he said.

Pepsi's iron ran over a lump in the back pocket of David's black jeans. Checking, she came face to face once again with the photos of Jacqueline Polanski.

"She is very white," she said.

"White? She's half Italian," David said.

"She is a ghost."

"Oh, no, she's real, don't worry," he said. "She's been bleached by the sun, that's the problem."

"She is the one who sent you here."

David held the photo close to the light. "Yes and no," he said.

"She is pushing you, so you come here and pull my father," said Pepsi. "I don't like it."

"Too bad!" For the first time David's hard stare beat hers back. For the first time she held onto his gaze for half a dozen beats of his heart. She was strong as an elk, he thought, with skin as smooth as melting.

"I'm sorry," he said. "Tomorrow, I guarantee, I'm outa here."

A moment later, she asked him what he wanted to do with his life. It was innocent enough but it scared him. She told him that her mother was born at a town called Livingstone, or so the colonialists called it. She frightened him, not because she was so close but because from the look in her eye she was getting closer, though she didn't move an inch. Her father, she told him, had promised to take his wife's final regards back home to Mosi-O-Tunya, only a mile from this place called Livingstone.

David wondered why she was telling him this. Did she want him to leave or not? He left the photos on the ironing board and backed away into the shadows, all the way to the Mercedes where he reached into the engine with the dipstick and felt around for the slot. Finding it, he guided the slippery tip into its sheaf and sank it into the engine block up to the hilt. He remained there under the hood hiding from so many pushings and pullings.

Pushing and pulling — those were the words Pepsi had used. They struck him the way a new song can hook you, the way a catchy phrase is repeated and repeated until the simple truth of it resounds with something personal and gets hard-wired into your belief system. The point of it was that he felt pulled or pushed by his own father, even though he was dead. Maybe haunted was the word he should use. For years he'd believed that his father's leaving took courage — that he hadn't taken his own life but had set out to live for the first time. David had decided that his last act had been a gift to him. Coming here was beginning to feel like an honouring of that gift. Maybe Pepsi worried about the rising tide in her own father's soul, worried that she would have to honour it as well.

The next morning dawned even chillier — cold for Africa, David thought. He snuggled under the covers on the tool shed floor until he heard a horn blaring and the squeal of brakes.

"Tobias Changwe!" It was the irrepressible Sergeant Angel Bukoba again. "Get dressed! It is time to pay for your sins!"

David kicked off the blankets and dressed quickly while listening to Bukoba imitate a vengeful judge.

"You are charged with driving without a licence, *Mzee!* What have you to say?"

David looked through the crack in the door. Bukoba stood on the running board of an open military Jeep, leaning on the horn, while Pepsi knocked on the door of her father's hut.

"I am a simple man," said Bukoba, making fun of Changwe. "Only doing my duty, your honour."

David pocketed a wrench and searched the shed for plastic lard buckets. Bukoba could try for a million years, thought David, without accurately mimicking the goodwill that issued from Mr. Changwe with his every breath.

Bukoba switched roles again to judge, back to Changwe, then to judge again. "But, Tobias, you disobey the law," said the serious Judge Bukoba. "But, your honour," said Mzee Bukoba, "Is it forbidden a one-legged man — ?"

Judge Bukoba interrupted, "People say Changwe builds a car to travel to faraway places. They say he retires like his rich cousin, the Highways Minister."

When Changwe appeared in the doorway, dressed and pressed and ready for judgement day in his banker's suit, Bukoba stepped off the running board, as sober as if he'd been slapped. David darted behind the Jeep and crawled beneath it. He found the plug for the oil pan and turned it with the wrench.

"The court says Changwe stays in Tunduma village and pays fine of ten thousand shillings for selfish dreaming." Bukoba continued his act, but in the face of Changwe's fashion statement, his convictions had lost their power.

As David waited for the oil to fill the buckets he could see only feet. One foot in particular caught his attention — it wore one of his cowboy boots and it moved with the aid of a crutch toward the Jeep and clambered aboard.

"More important than suits and ties, Mzee, is to get to court on time."

"I agree," said Pepsi. "Now we've heard enough from you. Please, belt up your mouth and drive."

David heard Mr. Changwe chastise Pepsi, and heard her issue her stock amend, "Please and thank you", before the Jeep started up and accelerated into a tight U-turn toward the trail. David rolled away from spinning tires and didn't move or open his eyes until the sound of the Jeep could be heard no more. He lay there for another few seconds wondering how long unlubricated pistons could keep pumping before melting red hot and fusing solid with the engine block. Then he carried the two buckets of oil to the Mercedes.

then drove into town. David watched Manon recruit those five men into pushing Bukoba's Jeep in the direction of Changwe's compound.

"I was a stranger and ye took me in!" Like a coxswain lending his rowers rhythm, Manon brought up the rear. "Naked and ye clothed me, sick and ye visited me, in prison and ye came unto me!"

David had work to do on the Mercedes but he didn't dare risk returning and being seen at Changwe's. By his reckoning the border town of Tunduma was less than half a mile away. If he headed that way, he might meet Changwe on his return. David was excited now that the Mercedes was coming together. When he saw Mr. Changwe he'd tell him that all they needed before setting out for the Zambezi was tires. With Sadarji and Albert in custody there a cage-full of tires waited to be had. The plan raced forward in David's mind almost out of control until it skidded to a halt when he saw Pepsi returning along the trail without her father.

"What happened?"

Pepsi was so furious and red-eyed from crying that she wouldn't look at David.

"What about the trial? What happened?" David nagged her until she exploded, as if the pressure of the disaster was so great inside her head that when it started to leak, it all came gushing out.

Her father had been humiliated, she said, in front of everybody. But especially the magistrate, whose green beret and khaki army jacket bedecked with slabs of bars, badges and war medals struck fear into all hundred and fifty citizens who had gathered under the mango tree. Pepsi wanted David to understand that in this country a person lived by the honour and the respect you earned amongst your neighbours. How much respect could be left for her father now? The whole village had watched while he removed that lizard skin cowboy boot and placed it on the magistrate's table as Exhibit A, along with Exhibit B — the credit card — and one of those incriminating Wanted Posters.

"The credit card? What about the car theft?" David said.

Pepsi turned on David, unable, it seemed, to find words strong enough to denounce him. "Tobias Changwe, it is charged that on the morning of September twelfth," said Pepsi, acting the judge, "you did harbour, and, indeed, are still harbouring a fugitive from justice. How do you plead?" Pepsi explained how her father had looked to her for guidance but how she'd remained silent, fearful of provoking an outburst, not only from the judge but from Sergeant Bukoba who suddenly appeared, standing at attention behind them.

"Thank you, David Livingstone," Pepsi said, "for ruining our lives exactly as I knew you would."

The sound of an approaching vehicle sent David running for the trees. At the wheel of a military Land Rover sat Bukoba, a one-man war in search of a battlefield. Under canvas in the back rode a small battalion of soldiers. They blasted up the trail toward Changwe's domain.

David couldn't persuade Pepsi to run with him. What did she care, she said. Her life was already in ruins.

TEN

Before David reached Changwe's yard he heard it being ransacked. Outside the perimeter of the clearing he crouched behind a sofa that lay rotting in a patch of elephant grass. From there he watched soldiers drag beds from huts and hurl mattresses into the dirt. They dismantled every appliance, flung clothes around the yard and levelled everything that stood on legs. Only two areas Bukoba declared out of bounds — Pepsi's dresser and Changwe's equipment shed. "Of great scientific importance!" Bukoba said of the gauging equipment.

Obviously, they were hunting for him, thought David. He wondered how he'd face the Changwes. It occurred to him that heading into Zambia through the bush on foot was a brilliant idea. He'd have better odds against the dreaded *mamba* than with Pepsi, because what possible antidote could there be to the venom of her wrath?

From his hiding place, David saw Manon standing amongst the debris looking at the Mercedes. He saw him open the Mercedes door and slip behind the wheel as if he was shopping in a showroom. At the sound of the door slamming, Bukoba stopped pawing through flimsy items in Pepsi's dresser drawer and walked toward the Mercedes. Bukoba should have noticed how the car had been cleaned, David thought, and how rust had been touched up with whitewash. As Bukoba approached the driver's window, the radio came alive with Wilson Pickett's "Mustang Sally". Then the engine rumbled, then sputtered, backfired and died.

"*Merveilleux!*" said Manon.

David's sentiments exactly. He watched Bukoba lean in the open window, drawn by Manon running his hand across the tan leather upholstery as if it was firm flesh. Something on the floor of the car on the passenger side seemed to catch Bukoba's eye and he tapped Manon on the shoulder and pointed to it. Manon picked it up — the other lizard skin cowboy boot. He handed it to the sergeant.

Bukoba ordered his troops into the Land Rover. He circled the yard in a victory lap, tires spinning. Seeing Pepsi arrive, he held David's boot in the air as if it was the head of an enemy chief, and headed for town.

David timed his entrance to the disaster area to coincide with Pepsi's. The only thing that moved in the yard was the Mercedes. It shimmied and growled as Father Manon revved the engine to find a harmonious level of rpms. He waved at David. David waved back.

With little apparent resentment, Pepsi began to repair the damage. She fanned the embers in the cooking fire and fed debris into the flames, including threadbare underwear, one old shoe, and dozens of those magazines that weren't damaged in the least.

It looked to David like a purge. What else could he do but keep his distance? He didn't dare ask, so he could only assume that Mr. Changwe languished in some kind of jail, still in his double-breasted Bond Street suit and worrying, no doubt, about the hour. It was almost four o'clock and time for his afternoon gauging of the river. For twenty years, Changwe had told him, he'd kept to a schedule that was unbroken except for reasons that God or the President would have forgiven him.

"We need three hundred thousand shillings for my father's bail," Pepsi said when David approached close enough to hear.

The Mercedes engine quit. Father Manon got out of the car, tapped the roof of the car as if he already owned it and said, "Hey, Sweetpea! How much?" he said.

Pepsi looked at David. He had nowhere to look except inside at his plans crashing around him.

"Three hundred thousand shillings," she said.

"Dat's a lotta dough," said Father Manon, "for a car without rubber. For a poor priest."

"Yes, I know, Father," said Pepsi. "But it is a lot of money they are asking for my father's bail."

David sat behind the wheel of the Mercedes and started it up. Manon stood at the open door expecting a sales pitch.

"This heap isn't worth half what she's asking," David said. He reminded Manon that hulks like this littered the countryside. Free for nothing.

Pepsi must have smelled trouble because she broke up their huddle with the claim that the car had a pedigree. Not only was it a Mercedes but it once belonged to a government minister. For proof, she opened the glove compartment and produced a small Tanzanian flag on a stick.

"Pepsi, it's got no wheels," said David. He couldn't come right out and argue on her father's behalf. He couldn't ask her what the heck was she doing selling it without his permission.

"Without tires," he said, "this thing is nothing more than a leaky boat."

"I tell you what," said Manon addressing Pepsi. "A hundred thousand. As is. Michelin, I'll get myself."

Pepsi shook her head. David got out of the Mercedes. He had to physically get between these two. He had to keep them apart. He had to be the bearer of more bad news about this wreck — the brake drums were rusty and the hydraulics were leaking. He dropped to his hands and knees and reached under the chassis to wet his finger on something oily.

"Two hundred thousand," said Manon.

David could see his efforts backfiring. He confessed that though the engine sounded okay, the transmission would drop into the first pothole the car drove over. He got behind the wheel and forced it into first gear to prove his point.

"Two hundred fifty thousand," said Manon.

David pointed out a battery that leaked, a tailpipe that rattled, windows that were cracked and lights that didn't work. Elephant grass was growing right up through the engine, for God's sake. Not only should this old beater be put out to pasture, said David, it had become pasture!

"Okay, okay. *Sacrament! Colis! Tabernac!*" yelled Manon. "Three hundred thousand!"

David appealed to Pepsi with a look that reflected all the fondness her father had for that car and all the dreams he had wound around it. She countered his nostalgia with a calculating and uncompromising stare and handed Manon the flag. Once again, David thought, it's women, not men, who are the pragmatic ones. He turned off the ignition. The engine stopped, convulsed, and stopped again.

"But Father, you're broke," said David.

"He will get," said Pepsi.

"Ask and it shall be given," said Manon.

"It'll nickel and dime you to death," said David, still trying to save Changwe's car.

"Seek and ye shall find," said Father Manon.

David knew the mad priest from Chicoutimi was no longer reachable. He was on a roll, inspired and prophetic, exalted and numinous. He could have sold Korans in St. Peter's Square.

"Please, seek quickly, Father," said Pepsi.

"Knock and it shall be opened unto you," said Manon as he rapped on the Mercedes' fender. The engine came to life for one final shudder, a shimmy that unseated the hood support and stopped when the hood crashed down.

David retreated to the river and the protection of the boathouse where he thought of his father — the loser. Sure, if you consider car rallying to be the end-all, then Errol had died short of his goal. But David knew that he was proud of what he'd accomplished. He'd confided in him — a son that loved him was all the victory he needed, he'd said. Just keep on loving me. David felt the same with Changwe. Car or no car, he loved the old man's dream of seeing Mosi-O-Tunya. Changwe's desire had crept into him, he thought, as sure as elephant grass grew through the engine of the Mercedes.

He remained in the boathouse and watched Pepsi as she measured the flow of the river. The Changwes had to live with the consequences, thought David, while his problems were those of a tourist. These events would rise like memory bubbles off the timeline of his life, then pop and be gone forever. Did it matter if he turned himself in or broke through the border or remained huddled like a water rat in this shed for the rest of his life? Thoughts like these bounced around the inside of his skull until they triggered an explosive fantasy — the ultimate road race featuring a four-wheel drive Gelandewagon hurtling over a sand dune, hell bent for somewhere near Timbuktu. Errol's dream. David, the keeper of other people's dreams, would never get it out of his mind.

Pepsi hauled the boat up the bank to the boathouse.

"Okay, listen," said David. He hadn't thought about what he was going to say but suddenly he was full of ideas. "I know a Mr. Ngoma. He's a big shot with the government."

"I know very well Uncle Felix Ngoma," said Pepsi. She left the boat and headed up the trail to the yard.

"You mean the Minister of Highways?" David tied the boat, took a cautionary look upstream and down, then chased after Pepsi, demanding to know if she was referring to "his" Felix Ngoma.

"He is the one who litters my father's yard with broken dreams," said Pepsi.

"Fantastic. He can bail him out," said David.

"Tell Uncle Felix for me," said Pepsi, "that because of him — and you! — my father will be taken to the capital and there he will die like a fish out of water."

"If you sell the car, your father won't care what happens to him!" David slowed to let Pepsi enter the yard by herself. He arrived a few minutes later with apology on his mind, but found Pepsi with basket in hand heading for the single-track trail that led to town.

"He can plead ignorance," said David.

"You think my father is ignorant," said Pepsi.

"No! About credit cards, I mean."

Pepsi stopped in her tracks, set the basket down and turned on David. "Yes, all right. If you are ready to face the judge and confess."

"Surrender, you mean?" said David. "Don't think I haven't thought about it. Ten times a day."

"Promise me, then," said Pepsi, "if this car, which you think is so bloody wonderful, which I am selling to raise my father's bail, is to be saved — promise me that you will surrender. To me."

"To you?" David asked. Of course, he thought. The reward. Why hadn't he thought of it himself?

"To be sure, you are not worth a hundred thousand shillings. But just this once, Pepsi will sell a false bill of goods for whatever the market will bring."

David had to think about it. It was an idea, all right. A good idea. But ahead of its time. It had to be. There had to be a way to cut the losses, to save Changwe and himself, and the car.

Pepsi retrieved her basket and continued up the trail, leaving David to chose between bad and worse.

ELEVEN

David promised himself that this would be his last day in Tanzania. He found a ragged cap in Changwe's equipment shed and took it down the hill to the boathouse where he bit more holes in it and inserted stems of grass. Wearing it, he submerged in the river up to his neck in the hope that passing bounty hunters would see only a floating clod.

Lying amongst the reeds like deadwood for the best part of the afternoon, David came unhappily to terms with the only honourable solution, which was, as Pepsi had suggested, to turn himself in and let the Changwe's reap the reward. While he floated in the river, he heard someone coming. His heart pounded until he saw Pepsi come to gauge the river. As she loaded gear into the boat, he tried to surprise her.

"You win," he said.

She saw him in the weeds. If winning didn't change her mood, the sight of him with a soggy grass hat should have.

"My father is losing his mind," she said. "I told him of our plan to collect the reward and he swore. He has never cursed. See what you have done to him."

Pepsi struggled with the clasps on the gunwale that hooked the boat to the cross-river cable. David saw that she was getting frustrated, so he waded toward her and helped her make the connection. He pushed the boat the last few feet into floatable water, hung on to the bow to steady it and helped her aboard. Her normally focused gaze was so dim that she didn't seem to care if she gauged the river or not.

"Do you ever see dumas from here?" David said.

"Pray you do not see the duma," she said.

"Is this where your father met the duma?" He hoped she would find comfort in family stories because, if her father had lost his leg to a duma, it only proved that he was a survivor, and would survive again. More than that, David wanted to hear about her connection with Mr. Ngoma. Was he really her blood uncle?

She sat in the boat looking drained as David walked her into deeper water. "They were just boys," she said. "So small to be in the jaws of the duma."

"It was the smell of fish on their hands, wasn't it?" David noticed her stiffen. What right had he knowing such details?

"My father watched from behind his mother as the duma held Uncle Felix," she said. She watched David as she spoke, hoping to see him flounder in the wake of facts he did not know, or so it seemed to him.

"Held him by the hand, right?" said David.

"Grandmother moved slowly but stopped when the duma growled. Grandmother made soft shushing noises to calm Felix because she feared the duma would taste fear in his blood. She spoke to duma, gentle words like a purring, I am told, and when she arrived at its ear she stroked its neck. She stroked the duma like a lover and massaged its throat. When the duma let go, Grandmother said to Uncle Felix, "Move slowly." Pepsi looked downriver.

"And then what happened?" asked David.

When Pepsi began again, her eyes darted about as if she was living the tragedy herself.

"She steps backwards and trips over my father who is hiding behind her. And the duma, he is startled and jumps on them, there by the river." Pepsi pointed downstream.

"Wow. So, he did get your grandmother."

"She picks up a stick to beat it away, for it is holding my father in its jaws. And the duma attacks her and they fall into the river together."

"No way," said David.

"The boys found her downriver."

"Dead?"

"Her face is terribly broken and she cannot open her eyes for all the blood. And her arm is hanging crooked. She tells Felix he must push her back in the river. She says, the duma will take her the rest of the way."

"Push her back in?"

"Felix could not. Could you?"

"I don't know."

"A little child cannot — even though she says her life is over. And she seems even peaceful but this is his auntie! He cannot kill Auntie. She tells him to take care of Tobias but, of course, what can a child even think about such things?"

"So, he didn't," said David.

"No. That is what I am saying."

"Mercy killing," said David. "It would be mercy killing. Any judge would let him off."

"Auntie was enough judge for Uncle Felix. For two years she didn't want to see him, so much pain she lived with."

"Meanwhile, your father is bleeding to death."

"Little Felix carried him on his back, running all the way to the village. It was a miracle, they say."

"So, Mr. Ngoma did the right thing. They both lived."

Pepsi took hold of an oar and lowered it overboard to give the boat a push, but David hung onto the boat.

"My grandmother did not call it living. And since, now, you know everything, I can tell you that one day she vanished. People say she finished herself what the duma should have finished there by the river. But do not ask me to explain things like "fate". I hate the word. No one can explain it to me. My uncle, he is so brilliant, but he least of all can explain. Fate visits us in cruel disguises, is all he can say. Now, if you don't mind, I am late."

Pepsi removed David's hand from the gunwale but David caught her hand.

"Fate. I hate it, too. We don't have to believe in it, you know. I wouldn't be here if I'd let fate run my life."

They looked at each other and for the first time David recognized common ground between them. David let go of her. She pushed on the oar and moved into the current.

"Did you know Father had three boys?" she said. David shook his head. "Three boys before me. They all died, one two, three."

At the sound of a low-flying aircraft approaching, David submerged. With strong strokes he pulled himself to the river bottom, then kicked towards the shore, losing ground against the current until he reached the reeds. He expelled some air and sank to the bottom where, for as long as he held his breath, he imagined the courage it would take to conspire with God about the day of your own dying.

By the time Pepsi returned from gauging, David had been watching her from within the boathouse for two hours. Once during that time, a soldier hailed Pepsi from the hill, asking her if she'd seen any strangers. David had pulled a tarp over himself as she called back, "Nay!" Now, finished on the river, she pulled the boat to the doorway of the shed.

Something had changed, either with Pepsi or himself. Tension remained, yet their antagonism had gone. Perhaps he now knew too much. Perhaps Grandma was sacred territory and because he'd shown interest in her story, Pepsi had to treat him with more respect. She crouched by the boathouse entrance and said she'd return later when the soldier left. They would discuss how they would arrange the end of her father's ordeal and bring him home. When she got up to go, her dress rode high on her thigh before it fell again to her knee. David noticed every inch of dark muscled leg. He looked away but found himself bombarded with mental images of her, all filtered through a dense screen of wishful thinking that took his breath away.

When Pepsi returned, she came with roasted chicken and corn meal but no lantern. They ate by twilight that reflected off the river, ate with their hands, mopping up the juices with a dry corn porridge she called mealie meal. One of the drumsticks was broken. David picked it up before Pepsi noticed so that she wouldn't have to relive the memory of Bukoba running that chicken down with the motorcycle.

104

They decided that he would turn himself in tomorrow morning. But he would need a disguise so that nobody could hijack him en route and claim the reward themselves. Pepsi had shoe polish, a dress and a shawl. As a woman, he would be low in social status, she said, almost invisible. The thought of David in Pepsi's clothes caused them to share a little laugh until she caught him staring at her body.

"Has your goddess at home no breasts?" she said.

"She might," said David. "I wouldn't know."

"I have heard that American boys are either obsessed or repressed or both. Which one are you?"

"Sorry?" David said.

"Don't be sorry. There's nothing sorrier than a sorry one," said Pepsi, picking up the empty dish and retreating to the water's edge to rinse it.

"Okay, I'm not sorry," David said.

Pepsi finished rinsing the plate and set off up the hill without another word.

"You're beautiful. If you want to know the truth," he called after her. She kept walking.

He wanted to shoot himself. He'd thrown their whole relationship out of whack with that little stab of honesty. He wanted to go after her and explain. Explain what? He'd told her the truth. The ball was in her court, which was fine except he didn't know the rules of the game. He and Jackie had made a deal — no sex. In her words, it was too complicated. He never plumbed the depths of that excuse, so it took on a secret life of its own in the unlit recesses of his sex-starved brain. "Sex was complicated."

Pepsi, on the other hand, was not complicated. She oozed "wherewithal", the quality that gives someone the confidence to move forward in their life. If David was short of anything, it would be wherewithal. Hearing someone approach and sure it could be no one but Pepsi, David vowed to keep his mind off sex and firmly on wherewithal. She came carrying a blanket.

Her gait had lost much of its arrogance and her rhythm some of its confidence. She now wore black, which might have explained why she looked different, blending into the night as she did. She crouched in the doorway, a solid black silhouette against a moonlit river.

"What happens to this bail money when my father returns for trial?" she asked.

"You get it back," said David.

"We will send you half," she said.

"What for?"

"It is you who turns yourself in," she said.

"Forget it. I'm outa here, no strings attached." He caught a whiff of something and realized that Pepsi wore perfume.

"I will keep you company for a few minutes," she said. She crept inside the doorway, laid the blanket down and made room on it for them both.

"I could stick around for a few days," said David.

"I'm afraid they will take you to Dar immediately."

"Who's going to testify for your dad? Who's going to prove he wasn't hiding me?"

"I will," she said.

"Oh, sure, they're going to believe you," he said. "Anyway, I doubt if you can lie as well as I can."

"For my father, I could kill." Pepsi's spine straightened. David reached out and took her hand.

106

"I'll tell them anyway," he assured her. "I'll make a statement. My mother's a lawyer. She can send something official from home, don't worry."

David let go of her hand but then Pepsi took hold of his and held on. She leaned toward him and lay her head on his shoulder. David let his eyes wander over her body, especially where the moonlight made stark smooth mountains out of her breasts. He put a hand on her shoulder and pulled her closer. His heart pounded. How could she not feel it?

"We cannot have sex," she said.

"That's okay," he said.

"It is?"

"We hardly know each other," he said.

"I know people who have sex without knowing each other's names," said Pepsi.

"Yeah? Well, I suppose that's okay but — I think it should be — spiritual. Don't you?"

"What are you talking about?" she said. "Some day I shall be married and it is better to have — to have a clear conscience."

"You're right, it could get complicated," he said.

Pepsi looked up at him. "Boys who like cars more than girls are not complicated at all," she said.

While David checked that out against himself, she kissed him on the mouth. It was a quick and uncomplicated kiss.

"Such boys are a bit simple, in fact," she said. She waited for David to deflate, then giggled, which proved she was just kidding.

David smothered her laugh with another kiss, this one more serious and possibly complex. Her eyes closed and she sank to the ground with him kissing her all the way.

He felt her whole body surrender and knew that he could have her. His hand instinctively moved to her hip bone. It felt like the safest way to get serious. Then his fingers slid across the fine weave of her black cotton dress to her belly and to the mass of soft, firm flesh of her breast. When he touched her nipple she giggled, so he slipped to her other breast and took that peak between his fingers and squeezed gently. Pepsi opened her eyes but gave him no clue of her yes or her no. He returned to her belly where he let his palm float until the current delivered him to the island of her pubic mound. She giggled again and took his hand.

"You should have been there," said Pepsi. She laughed out loud.

David shushed her and whispered, "Where?"

"At the court, when Angel Bukoba did not show up on time. The magistrate blamed the elders, the elders blamed each other."

"He wouldn't leave his Jeep," said David. "I was there."

"I don't blame him," said Pepsi. "But with no witness, the magistrate told the court there is no proof of my father's crime."

"Did he actually steal a car?" David asked, easing his weight off Pepsi for a better look at her.

"Of course. And His Honour, he knew of it." Pepsi had been talking into the darkness above her but now she faced David, all the better to impress upon him how powerfully the judge spoke. 'I have heard about it in Mbeya,' he said in his big voice," she said. "And he had earlobes just as big that wobbled. 'I have heard about it in Arusha! They are speaking of this in Dar es Salaam!' The crowd started to mumble angrily. My father could not look up. The judge said, 'a man with one leg wants his driver's licence!'"

David put a finger to her lips and listened into the silence outside. "Then what did he say?"

"He stood up. He announced that a man with one leg is building a Mercedes to see the world. People shook their fists."

"Didn't your father get a chance to speak?" David raised himself onto one elbow as if, by seeing all of Pepsi, he'd be a better witness to the drama that had unfolded.

"I promise to go no farther than Mosi-O-Tunya, your honour. That is what he said," said Pepsi.

"He's so honest, isn't he?" said David. He took hold of Pepsi's hand that rested now on her breast.

"The magistrate seemed to struggle with the very idea of a man with one leg going to Mosi-O-Tunya. He stepped out from behind the table which reminded everyone what a tall and distinguished man he was. 'A man with one leg builds a car and goes to Mosi-O-Tunya!' Everybody laughed. My poor father. The magistrate brought his gavel down with such a bang that blackbirds flew from the mango tree." David felt Pepsi's hand tighten into a fist. "Then, this proud old man with many medals, he pulled up his pant leg to reveal a wooden leg of his own."

"No way," David said.

"Oh, David, it was so quiet, as if everyone had been shot. The magistrate shook my father's hand. 'Such men are a credit to our nation!' he said. 'May God go with you.'"

Pepsi rolled into David's chest and started to cry.

"So — why is he in jail?"

"The petrol. The petrol my father had used up. It was only the matter of the petrol to be paid for," said Pepsi. "Eight hundred shillings and we were free to go."

"Okay, so?"

"As I looked in my purse, Father handed the magistrate your stupid credit card."

David felt Pepsi stiffen but he held her so that she couldn't roll away. Although she relaxed again as he stroked her head, whatever siren song she had been singing to draw him near had ended.

TWELVE

D avid woke at daylight to the sound of a car engine. He nudged Pepsi, pulled on his trousers and crawled under the boat tarp.

"*Mon pays, ce n'est pas un pays, c'est l'hiver* . . ." David stole a peek and saw Father Manon wading into the river wearing nothing but a red, white and blue Montreal Canadiens hockey jersey and singing the unofficial Quebec national anthem. His black frock, helmet, goggles and black leather riding boots lay on the hood of the Mercedes which sat by the shore.

"Pepsi, he's got tires," David whispered. "That's your dad's car. With tires."

"I will tell him the car is not for sale," she said.

"Good — good — " He kept saying "good", because a very good idea crystalized in his head as he spoke. And the farther Manon ventured into the river, the more plausible it became.

"I'm going," David said.

"I will get ready," said Pepsi.

"No, no, I'm going alone," he said.

"And how am I to collect the reward?" she said. "Or have you forgotten?"

David caught her arms as she tried to wrestle her way past him. It was urgent, this plan of his, and critical that Manon did not know they were there.

"Or have you lied to me so that I have slept with you?"

David muzzled her and begged her to listen but Pepsi bit his hand and spoke in angry whispers. She reminded David that his face was so famous by now that he couldn't go anywhere. He smiled slyly because his scheme took that into consideration. She slapped him out of frustration. If he was a real man he would honour his word and let her turn him in. He grabbed her arms so she couldn't smack him again and told her that his plan involved a disguise, a much better disguise than a floating clod, and it would begin the minute Father Manon walked far enough into the current that it carried him downstream. A distant rumble of thunder accompanied Manon as he headed for the rapids.

With the sinister black riding boots, David began his transformation into a priest. A car horn from Changwe's yard forced him to hurry. It also curtailed Pepsi's attack on him as she ran uphill to see who had arrived. David found the Mercedes keys in the ignition but he didn't dare start the engine. He couldn't wait too long, either, because Father Manon would soon be back. He approached the homestead through the bamboo patch until he had a view of the yard between two of Changwe's sheds. He saw Mr. Ngoma holding a pile of newspapers and magazines, and behind him, embassywoman Wilson.

The Highways Minister dropped the newspapers on the coffee table and forced Pepsi to take a good look.

"Canadian Missing on Hell Run!" Ngoma announced, as if she couldn't read. "And naturally, who is to blame? Ngoma, that's who! Look here, I am mentioned. I am quoted. I am bloody well hung out to dry!" Pepsi picked up the Dar Express. David could see his picture on the front page.

Mrs. Wilson stood aside looking astonished at the eclecticism of Changwe's yard. She took it all in from one spot, like a radar dish, until she moved to the cooking fire and pulled something out. From where David crouched, it looked like the photos of Jackie, half burnt.

"It is said that everyone gets their moment of glory," said Ngoma, still forcing headlines on Pepsi, "But Ngoma, what does he get?"

"It is well known that my uncle serves his country well," said Pepsi respectfully. She held on to the paper with David's mug shot on the front page.

"I was interviewed by *Newsweek*! for God's sake. Do you know how long those magazines sit in doctors' offices in America? Ten, twenty years, I am told! Am I right, Mrs. Wilson?"

She approached Ngoma with the photographs, which he snatched out of her hand without examining them. He was busy searching the yard for something else. "Pepsi, what's missing around here? Speak up, girl!"

Pepsi remained silent and David could see that it only made Ngoma more suspicious.

"My own flesh and blood is implicated, and you, who have more wits about her than all the Ngoma's and Changwe's put together, cannot find words to confirm what I have assured Mrs. Wilson is the case — that this is all poppycock." Ngoma only now glanced at the photos of Jackie. "Aphrodite!"

"Nay, Uncle," said Pepsi. "Do not mistake a ghost for a goddess."

"What have you done with this Livingstone character? I have brought this — this woman! — five hundred miles to prove how foolish these rumours are and I have been made a fool of. Now what? I must make good my word, of course, and launch a full-scale search."

Pepsi turned away and stood with her arms folded by her uncle's Mercedes.

"And damn it all, girl, what on earth is amiss around here? Good Lord!" Ngoma spun around. "Pepsi! Where is my old Mercedes?"

Pepsi forced the front page of the Dar Express on him. "He has it," she said.

Ngoma grabbed the paper and smacked the picture with the back of his hand. "This boy is killing me!" he yelled. Pepsi grabbed the paper and sat in the driver's seat, holding David's picture close to her breast.

"But he is helping my father to live," she said. She slammed the door shut, locked all the doors and leaned on the horn.

Seconds later, David accelerated through the yard in Ngoma's old Mercedes, waving as Manon would have done. From the look on Ngoma's face, David guessed that Manon was no more welcome in these parts than he was.

Ten minutes later, when David entered the jail office, Sergeant Bukoba was gathering empty Fanta bottles and tidying papers.

"Father! Quickly! Help me to put things in order. A very important visitor comes to visit the district."

"I tell you what — you clean the prison, I clean up the prisoners," said David. "Confession time!" The Quebecois accent was not so thick nor the vocabulary as crude as Father Manon's, but as long as he left his goggles in place he could probably fool Bukoba. "You, too, son of Norbert!"

"Nay, I have no need of such things. I am a sergeant. And I order you to pitch in."

"Hey, why not everybody pitch in? After confession in the fresh air, everybody is going to feel so pure they make everything spic and span."

"Outside, Father?" said Bukoba. "Nay, I smell rain."

"And what is rain but the cleansing hand of God?" David hurried into the cell block accompanied by a timely peal of holy thunder. "Confession time!" he yelled.

Bukoba ran after him.

Mr. Changwe lay on his cot with his head under a blanket, dead for all anyone seemed to care. In the adjacent cell, Albert sat up and kicked his partner who was sleeping on the floor.

"The French *fakir!*" Albert yelled. Sadarji opened his eyes.

"Thief! You have stolen our tires!" yelled Sadarji.

Sweet justice, David thought, and he wanted to celebrate it, but he had an immediate problem — he had to get Changwe out of there.

"Under the roof of heaven the spirit can fly," David told the sergeant.

"That is why my jailbirds are inside under this roof of concrete, Father." Bukoba rattled the cage with his night stick to awaken everyone.

115

"On your feet!" he shouted as he unlocked Changwe's cell. "The Father says you must confess!"

Bukoba warned the priest that a soldier needs no religion. He poked Changwe with his crutch and announced that only the weak and the poor need religion.

David grabbed the crutch from Bukoba and told him that, without religion, no priest would marry him. Bukoba rubbed his chin as if he was searching the map of his life for a shortcut.

"The gates of heaven can open to one who is baptized," said David. He spread his arms as the thick smell of warm rain wafted in from outside.

Bukoba seemed to delight in the concept of "heavenly gates", all the more as David opened his arms wider, making sure there was no mistaking his erotic double entendre. With Bukoba on his hook like a spring salmon, David told him he'd also have to confess his sins. When Bukoba opened his mouth to interject, lightning flashed outside and thunder crashed like a second story collapsing on the roof. Then the phone rang in the office. As Bukoba hurried to answer it, David called for a witness to the baptism. He took Changwe by the arm and helped him to the open cell door.

Sadarji gripped the bars and cursed "Manon" to hell and back for stealing his tires. David wanted to reveal himself to Changwe but Sadarji put up such a fuss that he stayed in character long enough to give the Sikh a piece of his mind. He wanted to repay these bastards for all the trouble they'd caused him since the day he arrived in this country, so he funnelled his vengeance through the filter of his Father act and out flowed a sermon about abandoning the highways of greed and discovering the river of goodwill that flows home. It was good stuff, if spurious nonsense. David started to enjoy it, even began to believe it as Sadarji stopped growling and sank to both knees. David finished up with an appeal to abandon old habits that keep you prisoner. "Your heart will save you," he said. It had wings and would never let you down.

Of course, David was talking to himself, making sense of the craziest days of his life. It reminded him of what MacGregor had once said — how he taught in order to learn, and wrote books in order to find out, and travelled to the heart of chaos in order to cultivate inner stillness.

David held out his hand so that the shamefaced Sadarji might kiss his hand through the bars, which he did. Sadarji's sincerity and his reluctance to let go touched David — until he realized that the Sikh had no intention of letting go.

"You!" shouted Sadarji. He pulled David hard against the bars and wrapped his rope suspenders around his neck. "Wolf in sheep's clothing! Stealing my tires! I will kill!"

The irony of it came home to David as he choked. Lightning, thunder, Sadarji screaming "Father of lies!", and Mr. Changwe raising his crutch above his head like a pick axe — all this violence became inconsequential to David as, inside, he grew strangely peaceful and logical. He wondered how much worse death might have been if Sadarji knew who he was actually killing. To David, it all unfolded in slow motion like a dance for the entertainment of angels who would soon be coming for him. He saw Mr. Changwe arrive at the top of his backswing and wince in pain as if he'd pulled a muscle. There was nothing for David to do but be grateful for the chain of events that had brought him to this crescendo and to marvel at lightning that bolted around the cell block like an electrical storm in a sci-fi, worlds-in-collision encounter. Pink bolts of light arced from Changwe to David as if they were a pair of dying solar systems combining their final charge for one last moment of brilliance. David grappled with the rope around his neck and off came his goggles, which didn't help him breathe but which made Sadarji pause and reconsider exactly who it was he was strangling. In that pause, Changwe discovered who he was saving and brought his crutch down hard through the prison bars and hammered Sadarji on the forehead. David fell free.

"Attention!" Bukoba shouted from the office. "The Highways Minister is soon arriving in Tunduma!"

David reinstalled the goggles over his purple face and led Mr. Changwe outside where a tin canopy protected the jail's porch from a downpour — the perfect theatre for a baptism, David told Bukoba. He arranged initiate and witness facing the doorway with their backs to the parking lot, though Changwe stole more than one proud glance at his Mercedes.

"Do you believe in God the Father, Angel Bukoba?"

"Surely, surely," said Bukoba, "But quickly."

The sounds of prison bars being ripped from their moorings could be heard within the cell block.

"And do you believe in Jesus and all the rest of that stuff?" asked David.

"Aye, Father, I believe," said Bukoba. "Just as I believe that the Highways Minister, who will be here any minute, will someday be the President. Aye, Father, I believe."

"Okay, okay. Come here." David led Bukoba to a forty-five gallon drum that overflowed with water streaming from the rain gutter. He placed a hand on Bukoba's head and encouraged it downward to the surface at the same time as he gave Changwe a nudge toward the car.

"Let's hear your confession, Bukoba," said David, forgetting for a moment his Quebecois accent, "And it better be good."

"Father, such bad words I have used in front of the Mzee. Please forgive such talk for, truly, Bukoba respects our water man."

"*Tres bien!*" said David. "I baptize thee, Angel Bukoba, in the name of the Father — " David let him straighten up only a few inches before initiating his descent again. "I baptize thee in the name of the Son — " David forced the sergeant's face underwater and held him there long enough for Changwe to get into the car. "And in the name of the Holy Smoke."

This time he dunked the sergeant past his ears and kept him down until Changwe started the car. Bukoba spluttered then pushed himself backwards out of the barrel, cracking his head on the door frame. He collapsed to the floor of the porch as white dust drifted out from within the cell block along with victorious shouts from Sadarji and Albert. Then, as if the jail had imploded, concrete dust mushroomed through the doorway.

David saw all this from the Mercedes as he and Changwe escaped. The last thing they saw through the rain and the smoke was Sergeant Bukoba getting to his feet while, in the doorway behind him, an apparition loomed like the Michelin Man risen from the dead.

"Petrol, Mr. David," said Changwe.

David knew they wouldn't get far without a pit stop. He pulled up to the pumps at the Tunduma Shell Station and rolled down the window to find an orange-uniformed pump jockey running toward him through the rain.

"Start pumping!" David yelled. "And hurry!"

"Yes, please," said the kid.

David closed the window against the rain but didn't dare look at Mr. Changwe who pressed his hands flat on the leather dashboard so that he could feel the pulse of the living engine. David didn't want to hear from him before they were over the border, didn't want to know about any last-minute doubts that must have been nagging him. At the same time, he didn't want to railroad Changwe into anything.

"Pepsi understands, Mr. Changwe, don't worry."

David opened the window and told the kid to pump faster. He let the rain soak his face rather than risk hearing his partner agonize over abandoning his duties. David saw the pump jockey coaxing one last litre into the gas tank.

"Enough!" yelled David. "We're late!"

As the attendant hung up the pump and screwed on the gas cap, David revved the engine and shifted into first gear, but he couldn't escape before the kid appeared at the window jotting a tally on a notepad. A map, that's what David wanted now. He asked for a map of Zambia, the biggest map he had, all of southern Africa if possible. As soon as the kid took off through the rain toward the office, David gripped the wheel and told his partner to hang on. Changwe grabbed his arm. David slammed the gas pedal to the floor and the Mercedes took off with a great whining of hot rubber on slick concrete.

"I should gauge my river, Mr. David," Changwe said.

"No, Mr. Changwe! Even the President gets a little time off!"

David could make out the Zambian border station a hundred yards away. He wished he hadn't said, "President". He knew it would remind Changwe of Nixon, and he was right. Changwe said that the American people felt betrayed by Nixon, were angry at him, yet he only did what he had to do.

"Listen to me," David said. As he slowed for the border, he could see a soldier draped in a rubber poncho, standing in the doorway of the hut. "I know about Nixon, okay? We studied him in school. He got swept out of office by a flood of public opinion. He fought history, kicking and screaming. But you're going with the flow, Mr. Changwe. And I'm with you!" He set his goggles over his eyes as he came to a stop beside the hut.

"God, he likes those who tell the truth," David told Changwe, his Quebecois accent now in place along with the disguise. He told Mr. Changwe to stay put, then he jumped out.

"Prison break!" he yelled.

The guard asked for his passport but David wanted inside, out of the rain, not an unreasonable request, David hoped, coming from a Holy Man.

Inside, a soldier with his head under a towel inhaled steam from a blackened pot as he talked on the phone. David told them to quit tying up the phone lines and find out about the prison break. The instant the sergeant hung up, the phone rang. It was Bukoba on the line and he confirmed everything.

"The prison is compledely broke!" the sick sergeant announced to his corporal. Sentence by congested sentence he relayed everything Bukoba said. "He is tied up! He dialled the phode wid his node!"

Bukoba ordered the border closed, the escapees arrested, their truck impounded, and someone to come and untie him immediately. The sergeant assured Bukoba that the border was sealed as of this very minute, but then a sneezing attack forced him to drop the phone. The corporal glanced outside. "What truck?" he asked.

"Arrest a priest?" said David. "You cannot arrest a priest!"

The sergeant looked outside then examined David for the first time. Looking back into the sergeant's rheumy eyes made David's own eyes water. He wanted to call him "Sneezy".

Confused and shivering, Sneezy picked up the phone again, but, before he could dial, the sound of an approaching vehicle sent him back to the doorway to see the tire truck accelerate past the hut, smash through the metal border gate and carry on full bore toward the Zambian gate fifty yards away. The corporal raced toward town in a Land Rover, leaving his sergeant to cope with another violent sneezing fit. Between convulsions, Sneezy ordered David to produce his passport. David suggested conducting business in the car where it was warm. But socializing with civilians while on duty was against regulations.

"*Mais, non.* The Mercedes is government property," David said. "Get in."

Too sick to argue, the sergeant got in the back seat. He wasn't so sick, however, that he couldn't draw a pistol and arrest Mr. Changwe the second he saw him. David told the sergeant to save his diseased breath. Mr. Changwe was already under arrest, not only according to Tanzanian law

but in the name of a much greater power. Whad power?
Sneezy wanted to know.

"The power dat make the rain to fall, Sergeant," David
said.

The sergeant looked upwards to the sound of the deluge
pounding on the roof but the pistol remained trained on
Changwe.

"The power that make the grasses grow and the trees
to become green with little baby leaves," continued David.

"It makes ganga grow," said Changwe.

"Ahh," said the sergeant.

As total understanding washed over the sergeant's face,
David drove slowly forward past the broken barrier.

"It is the power dat make the river full to overflowing,"
David said, winking at Changwe.

"Stop!" the sergeant yelled. "Where are you going?"

"Such a magnificent flood there is going to be,"
Changwe said.

"A flood?" asked the sergeant. "Where?"

"At Mosi-O-Tunya," said Changwe. A smile the size of
the chasm into which the mighty Zambezi was rumoured
to plunge, spread across Changwe's face.

David lifted his goggles and accelerated toward the
Zambian gate.

"Think of it this way, Sergeant — we're going after those
assholes who destroyed your gate."

"Faster!" yelled the sergeant.

THIRTEEN

O ne Zambia, one nation!" Changwe shouted as David drove past the Zambian border post without stopping. No one appeared from the hut to flag them down, nor could any trace of the border gate be seen. Mr. Changwe pointed to splinters of orange wood by the side of the road.

Finally, out of Tanzania and into the country that bore the name of the great river they sought — the Zambezi. It hardly seemed to matter that a Tanzanian soldier with a runny nose rode shotgun. What mattered was that the road they were on led west to the heart of the continent and that it now sped beneath them, mud, potholes, washouts, detours and all. It didn't pass beneath them fast enough for the sergeant, however. He wanted David to overtake a Zambian Police Jeep that pressed hard upon the tail of the tire truck. He reached over David's shoulder and pushed on the horn with the muzzle of the gun. When the truck swung wide on a slippery curve it gave the Jeep a chance to dart past. David accelerated in the Zambians' wake but never made it through before the truck hogged the road again on the straightaway and forced the

Mercedes onto the soft shoulder of the road. Stone-studded muck ripped the length of the undercarriage bringing them nearly to a halt. As David regained control, the engine growled like a vat of boiling lions.

"Sorry about that, Mr. Changwe," said David. "I think we lost the muffler."

"Apologizing not necessary, Mr. David. As long as the wheels go round we are doing our duty. To ourselves."

"I love it when you talk, Mr. Changwe."

"Can it be so?"

"It is so," said David.

"Then I must say that I regret being quiet these many years."

"Our loss, Mr. Changwe."

In the three minutes it took to catch up with the truck again, Changwe spoke non-stop about duties that kept him from seeing the world — a sick wife, children who died as babies, the last one taking his beloved with him, a daughter to raise on his own, and, of course, his commitment to his government job. All these obligations he put behind him, not as resentments but as reasons to demand his final reward.

"Bloody hell!" Changwe yelled as they saw the tire truck ram a vehicle from behind.

David could see that the Zambians were using their lead position to herd Albert and Sadarji to a stop. The truck slammed into the Jeep continually, forcing it to fishtail and sending it plunging into a drainage ditch. Sneezy pressed David at gunpoint to pass them, then fired at the truck's rear tires, but his target swerved to avoid a pothole, swung broadside and stalled, straddling the road. David braked, throwing the sergeant hard against the front seat. He jumped out, favouring his arm and wiping his nose as he ran toward the truck.

"You are under arrest!" The sergeant waved his trigger finger in the air. Though there was a finger, there was no trigger. That Sneezy didn't have his gun was clear to everyone. Albert cackled as he restarted his engine. David looked for the gun in the back seat and couldn't find it. Instead he saw a Land Rover approaching behind them so he pulled the back door shut with Changwe's crutch.

"Lock your door, Mr. Changwe."

Bukoba and the corporal jumped out of their Land Rover and ran past the Mercedes toward the truck, firing shots as they went. Sparks spit around the perimeter of the tire cage.

David reversed hard and stopped beside the Land Rover. He watched as Bukoba and the corporal ran after the truck, one on each side. David heard a gunshot and the sound of glass exploding. As the truck outdistanced Bukoba, he grabbed the cage above the tailgate and hung on, while the corporal twisted his ankle in a pothole.

Sneezy had also given up the chase to cough up something disgusting. He had run far enough, however, and was so crippled with fever that David could safely remove the keys from the Land Rover. The two soldiers could do nothing to stop David from driving past them except stand in the middle of the road. David had no choice, short of running them over, but to slow down, allowing Sneezy to jump on the fender and spread himself on the hood even as David accelerated to shake him off.

"Shit," David said. "Did you see that? He knocked the hood ornament off."

"We must be having an adventure, Mr. David."

"Adventure? This is a nightmare. This guy's like Spiderman all over the hood. I can hardly see the truck up ahead."

"When you wish you were not having an adventure," said Changwe, "that's how you know you are having an adventure."

"I'll know I'm having an adventure when I see you behind the wheel of this thing, Mr. Changwe. If there's anything left of it by then."

Bukoba clung to the truck as Albert tried to shake him off. He bravely made his way by increments to the top of the cage, then to the roof of the cab where he banged the butt end of his revolver on the roof. David couldn't see how this gave him the advantage because he remained at the mercy of Albert's driving. Two zigzags ripped Bukoba from his roof perch. He bounced off the right front fender and hit the road in a shoulder roll like a football player and somersaulted into the ditch. As David approached, he could see the sergeant holding his knee in obvious pain.

"Poor devil," said Changwe.

"Should we help him out?" asked David.

"Nay, Changwe is finished with such tiresome goodness." He pointed to the soldier on the hood. "He should help."

"Good idea. Hang on."

David slammed on the brakes. Sneezy rolled off the hood onto the road and scrambled on his hands and knees to the safety of the ditch.

After speeding away leaving the soldiers behind, David slowed to let the tire truck put some distance between them, then he stopped and got out. He circled to

Changwe's side, opened his door and pointed to the driver's seat.

"It's your car."

"It is illegal, Mr. David."

"All they can do now is hang us higher, Mr. Changwe," said David.

Changwe's smile revealed all his missing teeth. He shuffled sideways into the driver's seat and savoured the feel of the engine vibrations through the stick shift. He pressed the gas pedal to watch the tachometer rise and fall.

"Mr. Nixon —?," Changwe asked. "His chauffeur let him drive sometime?"

"Of course he did," said David.

With his one foot, Changwe tested first gear. He'd obviously practised engaging the gear slowly so as not to stall the engine. Switching his foot to the gas pedal required some skill because too much too suddenly would stall it again.

After watching Changwe discover second gear's range, David turned around and saw a plume of dust approaching behind them.

"Nixon — guess what he drove! Quick! A Porsche. A Porsche, Mr. Changwe! Make like Nixon!"

Changwe shifted to third at forty five miles per hour, then engaged fourth gear at sixty without using the clutch. David leaned back and, with great pleasure, watched Changwe smile and drive. It was an infectious smile and it made David want to whoop for joy. He leaned out the window to do just that and heard the buzz of a light aircraft low overhead. David craned his neck to get a good look at it.

"Cessna!" he yelled. "Call letters, Five-H, C-V-R!"

He settled back in his seat to watch it vanish out of sight behind trees.

"C-V-R. Thank God it's not Mr. Ngoma. He's Charlie Alpha Tango. I was in his plane. He's a maniac."

"You know my cousin Felix?"

"Kind of," said David. "C-V-R — what's that? Charlie something. V-R — what's that? Oh, shit! Victor Romeo. That's his highway patrol. Lose the main road, Mr. Changwe!"

The Hell Run had many breaks, many detours onto dirt tracks. Changwe abandoned the main road at the first opportunity. Recent rains had made muck pits of wheel ruts so Mr. Changwe cut his own trail parallel to the road.

"Not exactly two peas in a pod, you and Felix," said David.

"Quite right," said Changwe. "He can sing."

"He flies planes," said David. "He wears five hundred dollar suits; he uses big words."

"He won a scholarship," said Changwe.

"Philosophy, I bet."

"Cambridge Choir. There he learned about Karl Marx."

"He lives more like a capitalist. Like there's no tomorrow."

"Very true. Felix has learned that lesson well," said Changwe. "He tells me, 'Tobias!, do not count on tomorrow.' But I'm afraid I do. He is so good to me, I count on him visiting again and again."

"He was pretty good to me, too," David said. "But he likes interfering in people's lives, doesn't he?"

"Nay. I will tell you a story of the time he saved his auntie's life. He will never do it again."

"Oh, yes, he would."

"Nay, nay."

"He certainly saved my ass."

"Then you are as lucky as I, Mr. David. He will be your guardian angel."

David turned from Changwe to the window and another view of the sky.

The old road became so dangerous with ruts that Changwe abandoned it altogether and followed a game trail through dense bush until David told him to stop at the edge of a clearing behind an outcrop of rock. If they were visible from the air it would be only from directly above. When they could hear nothing but the buzzing of flies, they drove again, following the game trail from one meadow to another, scattering herds of grazing zebra as they went. They chased gazelles to a gentle height of land from where David felt for the first time in his life that he could see the breadth of the world and the length of a day. But nowhere could he see the Cessna.

Changwe aimed the Mercedes across a broad valley floor stomped flat and hard by herds of migrating wildebeest over millions of years. It was a highway all the same, thought David, built by animals who did nothing but answer to their heart's desires. It rode a whole lot smoother than Ngoma's precious Hell Run. Half way across the valley, Changwe veered away from a water hole but got stuck in jet-black muck on its fringes. David got out. Here and there, he saw collections of snow-white bones. A band of pushy vultures picked over a heap of remains. If not for their plucking and fluttering it would have been deathly quiet.

The water hole as source of life and death, David thought. Animals come here to drink and get stuck, just like Changwe's crutch was stuck in gumbo. David held him steady while he yanked it free, then left him to rest on the front bumper while he walked a few paces onto firmer ground and into a deeper stillness.

Wildebeest that had scattered upon the arrival of the Mercedes now returned to the pond, each one a clone of some ancient prototype, each one as ragged and ungainly as the next. David hoped that something more than dumb instinct coursed through his arteries. There had to be.

At the sound of voices, he turned to find Changwe greeting two barefoot men and a woman, hunters who approached carrying three live but subdued guinea fowl. Their clothes were worn limp and bleached colourless by constant wear under a tropical sun. They laughed as they greeted Changwe with great open palms. Seeing David, they dropped to their knees and bowed to the earth in front of him. David appealed to Changwe to do something. Embarrassed, Changwe barked an order that sent everyone into more fits of laughter as they rose to their feet. On an impulse, David dropped to his knees and bowed as they had done. The strangers howled so hard with laughter that one of the guinea fowl escaped. The woman chased it down while the men cut tufts of grass and wedged them under the Mercedes' tires. After five minutes of pushing, the Mercedes was high and dry again.

David took over behind the wheel, steering a route the hunters had described until they came to a stream they had no choice but to cross. The water was axle-deep except in the centremost section. David waded into the current and tested the depth with Changwe's crutch. The waterline, when he tested it against himself, came up to his waist.

"We can pass," said Changwe. "Like the water buffalo."

David geared down and raced the engine so that even as the car sunk to the bumper and water poured through holes in the floorboards, the fire in the heart of the German autobeest didn't die. The overheated engine vapourized any water that got near it and expelled it through every seam in the body of the car. Climbing out of the shallows on the other side, the tires screamed on hot gravel until they smoked. David let out a great howl, too. One close call after another over the last four days left him giddy from withholding emotion, and now that he had no reason to contain himself, tears streamed down his face. Nevertheless, he felt silly. After stopping on the other side, he assured Changwe that he was okay but the old gauge reader insisted on getting out to allow David a moment's solitude. Changwe pointed to his watch as if to say, it is the time of day to cry.

In the rear-view mirror, David watched him walk to the stream. Of course, he thought, four o'clock. Back home, Pepsi would be in the boat, torpedo spinning beneath the surface of the stream, clicks dutifully recorded in the book. For all David knew, Changwe was crying as well.

By sunset they had driven a hundred miles farther south to the ferry crossing of the Luangwa. Five men glistening gold with sweat powered the two-car raft by pulling as a team on a rope that stretched across the river. Changwe sat on the hood of the Mercedes and talked all the way across, entertaining the ferrymen with a story so rich but solemn it might have been an ode to all rivers. More probably, David imagined, it was Changwe's own Kalungu River he spoke about and its vital role in feeding mighty rivers like this one.

132

David sat on the bumper below Changwe and watched the way the men gripped the rope and heaved in unison. In the fading light, heading toward the safety of the far shore, David let his guard down enough to see how one minute you are running for your life and the next minute given over to the sure hands of others. Not only was the ride free but a ferryman made Changwe a gift of a dried flat fish wrapped in newspaper. And presented with all the respect of a warrior to his elder, David thought, or a son to his father.

They made camp by this river two hundred yards upstream of the ferry landing. The tropical twilight was short-lived but all the more intense for reflecting off the water. The far shore was not dark green any more but black, though still luxuriant. David could smell it. The light from their fire tickled the tawny grasses all the way to the river's edge. David and Changwe ate their fish skewered on a stick, then barbecued.

"This is hard for Changwe to understand. A one such as you did not want to leave home."

"Mom travels enough for both of us," said David. "Anyway, all you read about is war. Or famine or hurricanes. Not my idea of a good time."

"And yet you have journeyed so very far," said Changwe. "Is it that you have prayed to God as I have done?"

"Me? Are you kidding?" David chewed the last of his fish. Then he smelled his hands, licked them, smelled them again and walked to the water's edge.

"Many years ago I prayed to God to cool my thoughts," said Changwe. "I was such an angry one." He raised his crutch into the air to demonstrate how he might have fended off that cheetah if he'd been stronger.

"Your prayers must have worked," said David wetting his hands. "You wouldn't hurt a flea."

"After many years I prayed again for God to return the temperature of my childish dreams."

David scrubbed his hands with sand then rinsed them. "MacGregor, my teacher, that's who got me steamed up," he said. "And a duma name Jacqueline Polanski." David pronounced her name as if it helped him picture her clearly. Then he let her go.

"Changwe wishes he could go to such a school. Is it permitted one as old as I?"

David looked onto the opaque river, then into the translucent waters at his feet. Changwe at school?

"Why not?" David said.

There'd been a few "mature students" as they called them. They didn't dick around. MacGregor would love Changwe. He'd invite him to the blackboard every chance he got. "Changwe! Changwe! Changwe!" the class would chant. In David's fantasy, he saw Changwe at the blackboard proving mathematically why rivers don't run straight, why they meander aimlessly, for no reason. Changwe needs more space and by accident erases that familiar name in the corner. "Detention? What detention, Mr. MacGregor?"

"We'd drive to school in our Mercedes, Mr. Changwe," David said.

He removed the rear seat from the Mercedes — it was already loose — and installed it by the fire for Changwe's bed, but his partner didn't seem tired at all.

"Your MacGregor would send Changwe far away, as he has done to you, Mr. David," said Changwe, still standing. "Tobias, you go to Mosi-O-Tunya, he would say. You sit too long by your hut."

David laughed. He stretched out on the seat to watch Changwe continue in the skin of Mr. MacGregor. Changwe picked up a burning stick and brandished it at the onelegged schoolboy in his mind's eye.

"Tobias!" he mimicked. "You tell people that the duma taught you secrets. You read magazines and think you have travelled the world." David smiled but his eyes were closing. "Bullshit," said Changwe. David opened an eye. "Is it permitted such a word in class?" Changwe asked. "I have read that Nixon has said such things."

A carnivorous grumble emanated from deep in the night. Changwe waved his stick at the darkness.

"Duma, don't bother us! You have missed your chance! Now, we are masters of our fate, Duma."

David smiled but his eyelids drooped with sleep. Something about Changwe's round, kind face was like a father's arms around him.

FOURTEEN

David moves slowly down an unlit hallway. A floor-board creaks underfoot. In his hands, a three-foot catfish. Reaching a doorway, he nudges it open with his shoulder. The hinge squeaks. He listens for sounds of stirring upstairs, then enters the library and treads across a hairy rug toward MacGregor's oak desk. He opens a bottom drawer and lowers the fish in but it slips out of his hands and slops into the drawer, alive. David turns at the sound of a guttural purring. From high on a bookcase, three large cats leap toward him, arcing through the air one after the other in an orange blur.

David woke in a sweat. The darkness seemed wide awake. Embers hissed and popped as if a breeze had fanned the fire. The dream reminded him of a picture book he'd seen as a child. A tiger ran so fast around the base of a tree that it melted to butter. Little Black Sambo. Weird, a tiger turned to butter. David laid his head down again and closed his eyes. Butter. Butter on pancakes with maple syrup. He heard a grunt. Or did he? He opened his eyes and craned his neck to check on Changwe sleeping on his bed of cut grass. Cheetah! Over old Tobias stood the duma.

A hump high on the cat's back made its head seem small. Its long, lean belly hung taut between oversized hips and shoulders. Without taking his eyes off it, David reached for a stick in the coals but couldn't touch it without falling off the car seat. The cheetah locked onto his gaze. You don't stare down wild animals, David knew that, so he looked away, but he'd already seen everything. A black stripe ran from the corner of her eye to the corner of her open mouth. Three black rings adorned the end of her tail. She was savage but wholesome, like a fatal attraction. David flashed on Auntie and her wanting the duma to finish her off. When your Angel of Mercy shows up, he thought, it takes no prisoners.

In one seamless action David rolled off his bed, grabbed the smouldering stick and slashed a flaming hole in the night air. The flare blinded him to the blow that knocked him over and bowled him to the edge of the river. His torch rolled after him through grass creating a ball of wildfire that forced him backwards into the water. The duma exploded through the flames and leapt off the bank with her back arched and crushed him into the cold, fast depths. If this was drowning, why was he was being held, and why did they head toward a place that thundered? If this was death, he was committed to her strong arms. If he plummeted over the falls, if that's what this free fall meant, then goodbye, Jackie, thanks for everything, and I hope you loosen up a little bit when you fall in love again. Such matter-of-factness surprised him as he somersaulted through a rainbow, waiting for the end. David woke again. No cheetah, no rainbow. Still night.

He looked at his Ironman watch — 3:40. That's it, he thought. No more sleep tonight. A gust fanned the embers into a short-lived flare that illuminated the sleeping Changwe. David heard an explosive yelp and a staccato purring that could have come from near or far away, it was hard to tell. He moved the car seat closer to the fire and sat cross-legged and alert at the steep edge of sleep from where he could see anything coming from any direction.

After two hours, the eastern horizon bled with the first sign of tomorrow. Not yesterday, not quite a new day, what was this? David felt alone and strangely powerful as if victory and defeat were partners, as similar but different as our two hands, or a bird's two wings. The thought occurred to him that if he tried hard enough, he could fly.

The rising sun woke David again. Light filtered through the grass, warm and ochre. He surfaced from a sleep so deep that his dreams didn't find him before he noticed that Changwe and the Mercedes were gone.

The tire tracks made a clear impression through damp grass leading toward the main road. David found Changwe a hundred yards away, struggling up the river embankment. The Mercedes lay on its side behind him a few feet from the river's edge.

"Oh, no! What were you doing?"

"Parallel parking. Very sorry."

David saw two small logs spaced fifteen feet apart on the sharp shoulder of the road. Tire tracks disappeared over the edge. "I told you, Mr. Changwe! Didn't I tell you?"

When the old man lowered his head, David noticed blood trickling from a cut on his head. He slid down the slope to join him.

"Parallel parking, it's a bitch, I told you." He helped Changwe back to the shade behind the car and told him he'd be right back.

David ran to the ferry dock, anticipating that five strong men should be able to coax the Mercedes up the slope to the road. They'd have a rope for sure, and maybe even a vehicle to tow them. They'd come to the rescue because they respected Mr. Changwe and because, out here, *ujamaa* was a national attitude. All this wishful thinking evaporated when he saw that the ferrymen were gone and the dock stood empty. David looked across the river to see the raft loading its first trip of the day. The first vehicle across could tow them up the embankment, he thought. He shielded his eyes against the low sun for a better look at the ferry's cargo — two Land Rovers and a white Mercedes. David backed away and broke into a sprint.

He hadn't run a hundred yards when he saw, to his left, trucks parked behind trees on a roadside pull-over. Three hammocks hung between trees. Through a gap in the bushes he saw Sadarji urinating in front of his truck. David stopped. The sudden cessation of footfall caused Sadarji to turn. Seeing David, the Sikh made a noise like the combined bellows of someone pinching his testicle in a zipper and choking on a fish bone.

Before David had ran fifty yards, he heard the truck's engine roar. He scrambled down the embankment to find Mr. Changwe behind the car, knee-deep in the river, bathing his cut head.

"We're screwed!"

At the sound of the truck approaching and stopping on the road above, David retreated with Changwe into the river, protected from view by the overturned Mercedes.

139

Their only hope depended on Albert and Sadarji continuing to act out of blind greed. As the truckers descended the embankment to cannibalize the Mercedes, they'd be blind to David and Changwe slipping into deeper water. Under cover of feathery bamboo along the shore, they would wade upstream, climb the embankment, backtrack along the road and steal the truck. That's what they'd do and that's what they did, although the time it took David to start the engine and build up speed was time enough for Albert to scramble up the slope and jump on the running board. Changwe pulled Sergeant Sneezy's missing pistol out from under his belt and shoved it in his face. Albert raised his hands, teetered, then vanished from view forever.

Mr. Changwe aimed the pistol at the sky through the smashed front windshield — Bukoba must have shot the glass out — and pulled the trigger three times to no avail. He tipped the gun downward to let water run out the barrel, then threw it as far as he could into the passing *bundu*.

FIFTEEN

A mongst nuggets of shattered glass on the floor under the driver's seat, David found a map. He passed it to Changwe who had difficulty opening it in the wind that blasted through the broken window. David swerved to cut off a Zambian Police Jeep that tried to overtake them. In the side mirror he saw Ngoma's white Mercedes, and behind him another green Land Rover.

As they approached the foot of a hill, David looked for moral support in his partner's eyes but the light was gone. The throaty buzz of an approaching aircraft reached a crescendo as it passed low overhead.

"Take the wheel," said David.

When Changwe had two firm hands on the wheel, David climbed through the windshield onto the hood, then mounted the cab and pulled himself onto the cage. The Cessna circled and dove low enough to scare David flat on his stomach.

"David! You must stop! In my custody you are safe! Otherwise, I cannot guarantee!" Ngoma's voice crackled from a loudspeaker on the Mercedes. The message was clear, yet it seemed to come from far away. David wanted to shout, "What about the untamed heart, Mr. Ngoma!" but he saved his breath to climb down the back of the cage.

"David! Listen to me! In my custody, Tobias will be spared the consequences!"

The Land Rover pressed so close behind Ngoma that David could see Sergeant Bukoba wielding a pistol.

David wrestled with the latch on the cage door but it wouldn't budge except by degrees when the truck hit a pothole and shuddered. Tires piled up against the door as the grade of the hill increased. David used both hands to lift the bolt, then hung onto the cage door as it swung open. Tires escaped the cage like bombs from a dam buster, forcing the posse to slow down and pull over.

David clambered to the roof of the truck's cab where he could see Changwe in the side mirror. Tears ran down the old man's face.

As the truck crested the watershed and descended into another valley, David raised a fist at the Cessna overhead and at a helicopter that joined the chase. Though he and Changwe didn't stand a chance against a ground and air attack like that, there was something deeply satisfying about going all-out, something ultimate about leaving everything, especially your reputation, in the dust, far, far behind.

Something about the bridge up ahead made David drop to his stomach and lock his boots in the mesh of the cage and bang on the roof.

"Stop!"

Changwe hit the brakes. The pads smoked and the drums screeched but the truck didn't stop before it had skidded ten feet onto the bridge. The engine wheezed and died.

David could see that the far side of the bridge deck had collapsed into the river. Twenty feet below, a river churned through a small gorge.

"Reverse, Mr. Changwe." David heard the bridge creak. "Mr. Changwe! Back up!" David inched forward on the roof of the truck until he could see Changwe's hands on the steering wheel, knuckles white as barnacles. "Mr. Changwe?"

Changwe's eyes were open but they didn't see. David climbed through the windshield to take over behind the wheel but he froze half way as the bridge shifted, wobbled, then settled. David didn't breathe.

The Cessna approached from up the valley, its rpms cut back for a landing. The helicopter hovered lower and David could feel the chopper's vibrations in the frame of the truck. The instant David moved, something down below splintered, which released a succession of eerie groans. He retreated onto the truck's hood but felt the world listing, then he heard a prolonged screech that could have been the final agonies of a dying monster.

As the bridge deck collapsed, David fell against the abutment and hung on to a beam. He watched the torrent swallow the truck. The helicopter created a micro monsoon that lashed him with shards of grass and twigs and spray. The rotor's mechanical thwacking drowned out voices. Who was yelling? What were they yelling? Or was David imagining voices? It didn't matter because every cell in his body yelled, "Jump!"

He let go.

Six feet under, shifting shafts of jagged light danced through black water. David grabbed the truck's window frame before the current carried him away. He wrestled the door open and tugged on Changwe's arm but the old man's hands were locked to the steering wheel. As he detached each rigid finger, absolute necessity acted like an anaesthetic against his panic, but it also gave him the space to be astounded at how easy it would be to just choose death. He could just quit. It would be no big deal for either of them. His choice.

David surfaced, sucking water and air, but the dead weight of Changwe beneath him allowed only a second to catch his breath. His one glimpse of the riverbank recorded a snapshot of bedlam — Ngoma shedding his suit coat at the side of the river, Pepsi scrambling down the steep slope, and at the top of the bank, Mrs. Wilson watching, while behind her policemen jumped out of a Land Rover. Over everything, the helicopter's rotor wash beat on the scene like a rogue squall. David saw Ngoma catch sight of him, saw his mouth form the word *Tobias!* even before the sound came out. As Ngoma lunged for him, David went under again.

Holding Changwe left him helpless. Although an eddy in the current controlled him now, there was no question of letting go. He had come so far he wouldn't have recognized home if the river had tossed him onto his own doorstep. He felt a hand lock onto his arm. Solid ground beneath his feet allowed him to lift Changwe above water while Ngoma's other hand grasped him by the underarm, but they could do nothing but hold their own against the river, even as Pepsi grabbed her uncle's belt from behind and screamed for help. Seconds passed like hours as the foursome clutched each other like shipwreck survivors. David could feel Mr. Ngoma breathing, literally, down his neck.

"I'm sorry," said David. It felt like an apology to everyone he'd ever known.

A policeman relieved Pepsi as the anchor person, while another got a grip on Changwe. They hauled him to level ground halfway up the bank where they laid him on his side and checked for a pulse. Ngoma steadied David at the water's edge as he retched water.

"Pulse, yes!" yelled the officer taking charge.

As Ngoma ran to join them, David saw Mrs. Wilson standing nearby, staring at him.

"This may have started off as a prank, Livingstone, but you can bet CNN doesn't waste it's time with practical jokes." She pointed to the chopper overhead.

David moved past her to find the officer removing crud from Changwe's mouth before rolling him onto his back and beginning mouth to mouth resuscitation. Ngoma held his cousin's hand.

"He froze at the wheel," said David.

"Somebody should have told you," said Ngoma. "He has a bad heart."

Changwe coughed. The officer pulled back. Changwe opened his eyes and a cheer went up from everyone, including Sergeant Bukoba.

"Hospital transport!" yelled the officer.

"You are making big news, my cousin," said Ngoma, stroking Tobias' head. "Taking care of my little friend from far away."

"Little friend?" said Mrs. Wilson. Policemen pushed her aside and prepared to lift Changwe.

"You will soon be famous enough to run for national assembly," said Ngoma.

As strong arms hoisted Changwe, his eyes closed again. "We have enough of Marxists and Rhodes Scholars," Ngoma told him. "What we need now is the common man."

"Aye," said Pepsi.

The officers carried Changwe up the bank to a grassy flood plain where the Cessna "Charlie Victor Romeo" taxied toward them. Ngoma paused beside David and watched him shiver.

"You have caused me much trouble, David, but I will not deal with you now. There is only one thing on my mind."

"There's only been one thing on his mind for a long time," said David.

"I know what's best. I am his cousin! And I am in charge here. And your boondoggle is over!" Ngoma rushed ahead.

David hated feeling like this, powerless. He hated it! It made him hot, as if this guilt was just another old habit, burning, along with other outmoded habits that he'd torched in recent weeks.

"I'm not sorry!" he yelled.

He watched Ngoma speak to the pilot while the rescue party installed Changwe in the plane's passenger seat. Fifty yards away the media helicopter hovered above a landing, its camera crew at an open door ready to bail out. Mrs. Wilson, filthy from struggling up the riverbank, limped toward them waving a muddy shoe but turned away in the face of a blast of flying debris.

David joined the cluster at the Cessna to get a last glimpse of his old friend. Pepsi and the officer-in-charge continued to monitor Changwe's pulse, his breathing, and the temperature of his skin. The old man's eyes were closed, his head bent at an awkward angle.

"When you're airborne, Mr. Changwe, look south," said David. "You might see Mosi-O-Tunya. See if it's true what they say about Smoke That Thunders."

The pilot started the Cessna engine and executed his pre-flight checks. The vibration set up a jiggling in Changwe's limp body and he opened his eyes. David took his hand.

"I'll see you back there. We'll plan this thing out better next time, all right? No priests, no judges, no jails, okay? Just two lazy-ass tourists with a credit card. What do you say?"

Changwe smiled. David lifted his partner's hand into a bonding brotherhood grip and squeezed.

"Excuse me! Mr. Livingstone!" The reporter shouted from behind a rank of police officers. He was an American, overweight, sweating and dishevelled in a pink shirt, and desperate as if his career depended on this interview.

"Is it true you were so upset — ?"

A policeman ordered him back ten paces. Three officers formed a wall against him as Ngoma snugged Changwe's seat belt tight and kissed him on the forehead. His cousin's eyes had closed again and his head fallen to the side. Ngoma placed a palm on Changwe's forehead, then pressed fingers to his wrist.

"Good lord!" he said. "Medic!"

The officer checked Changwe's neck pulse, then placed an ear to his mouth. "Oh, no," he said.

Ngoma stopped him from undoing Changwe's seat belt and shook his head. The pilot turned off the ignition and removed his hat, then threw it against the windscreen.

While cursing under his breath, the medic crossed himself and retreated, moving past his men who, one by one, realized what had happened and removed their caps.

As the Cessna's propeller fluttered to a stop, Ngoma closed Changwe's door and put an arm over David's shoulder; Pepsi opened the door and sobbed on her father's chest. The reporter seemed to be the only one without any idea what had happened. He moved in again.

"Mr. Livingstone! Is it true you were so devastated at losing your girlfriend to your English teacher that you were going to throw yourself over Victoria Falls?"

Pepsi turned around, snatched the microphone out of his hand and threw it to the ground while Ngoma raised a hand to quell emotions.

"I have all the reason in the world to believe my cousin died a happy man," said the Honourable Mr. Ngoma. "Who amongst us would not give their right hand to die climbing the mountain in the shadow of which they have lived their entire life?"

David saw Mr. Ngoma look at his scarred hand on the way to closing the door against the prying eye of the camera. Then, once again, Ngoma faced the small crowd and the news camera.

"Tobias was a true pilgrim, living his simple yet honest existence in preparation for one great adventure. Let us hope, for our own sakes — because our time will just as surely come — that angels come to guide him the rest of the way. I have heard that it is so."

David saw Ngoma cast him an appreciative glance but he was in no mood for anything as half-hearted as thanks. David deserved to die right along with Mr. Changwe, didn't he? He'd killed him, hadn't he?

"Mr. Livingstone." As the journalist pressed forward, David turned on him, fists clenched.

"Dr. Livingstone, I presume," said the newsman. "Sorry, buddy. As a reporter I've always wanted to say that. Ha, ha, ha."

"Fuck you." David shattered inside. His words shook up the reporter, too, but not enough to squelch a professional muckraker. The American apologized then introduced himself as Howard Shatner, and proffered a deal for exclusive rights to David's story. Would he please step aside so they could discuss it?

Mrs. Wilson butted in. No way a fugitive was going to benefit from his crime.

"Madame, shut up!" said Ngoma.

Wilson looked around for support. Where moments ago a life and death crisis crystallized everyone's attention, now everyone melted away, Ngoma to his Mercedes to radio headquarters, soldiers and police to the baobab tree with a pack of cigarettes they'd scored from the chopper pilot. Even the Cessna pilot wandered off to piss by the river, leaving Changwe in the cockpit and Pepsi sitting like a samurai guard, cross-legged on the grass beside the plane.

If Shatner hadn't been dogging David to consider his deal, David might have collapsed, his knees were that shaky. He bent over for air, barely hearing what Shatner said because an umbilical cord still connected him to Changwe. It channelled so much unexpressed affection that David could have burst into tears, something he desperately didn't want to do. His heart pounded; panic gripped the artery that fed his brain so that he couldn't think. There was no question of sweet-talking this beast. No massaging its throat. He saw himself making a mad dash into the *bundu*, never to be seen again. Some people would call it suicide. He felt that if he straightened up he'd have to get a grip on something. Shatner's neck would do but then he'd probably kill him. Or Shatner's pen to sign the goddamn contract; what difference did it make? Or Pepsi, but she had her own problems, all his fault. The moment required another miracle and such things were out of his hands.

"Ten thousand dollars," Shatner said. "What do you say to that?" He had a contract ready to sign.

"Thirty." David blurted it out, thinking thirty thousand would shut Shatner up, but he accepted. David straightened up. He wasn't sure he'd heard correctly.

"US dollars," he said.

"Of course," said Shatner. "What did you think? Canadian?"

David signed the contract with a flourish and two definitive dots over "Livingstone" that stabbed holes in the paper. He told them to make the cheque out to Pepsi Changwe. Shatner moved David into shade under the Cessna's wing and signalled his cameraman to roll tape.

David found a new voice, a deep and forceful one, as he talked about being at a crossroads, about being confused by love and coming to Africa to get to the root of it. He described the characters he'd met and about finding a father figure in Mr. Changwe. He'd discovered something similar to love, he said, but less selfish, something less personal but more profound. In ten minutes he gave them a saga intended to rock the fence and anyone sitting on it. Shit or get off the pot was his message. Shatner said they couldn't use that part in prime time but he thanked David for the interview and shook his hand.

150

David let go of Shatner slowly, as if he now considered him an ally. He saw Sergeant Bukoba smoking and laughing with the other soldiers in the shade, and he respected the single-mindedness of his spirit. With so many other officials around, however, David noticed that Bukoba had let his guard down. He managed to slip into the pilot's seat and secure his seat belt before Bukoba appeared, running around the tail of the Cessna.

"You — !" Bukoba probably couldn't bear to hear himself arrest David one more time. He yanked the door open for David to get out.

"Sergeant, when your people learn what you've done, they'll carry you on their shoulders."

"Done? What have I done?"

"Pepsi will worship you for as long as you live." Bukoba looked perplexed. "No!" said Bukoba. "I will be arrested. You are arrested!"

A Zambian officer appeared and wanted to know if everything was okay.

"The judge with one leg will hear your case," David continued. "He'll acquit you. Even better, he'll sing your praises, Sergeant. He'll call you an Angel of Mercy."

Bukoba told the Zambian that everything was okay, then turned to see Pepsi watching incredulously through the passenger window.

"She will be happy, you say?" Bukoba whispered.

"Wouldn't you want your father's last wish to come true?" David said.

He said it loud enough so that Pepsi could hear. She brought her hands together at her mouth, which David interpreted as prayer.

"See those tears running down her cheeks, Sergeant?" said David. "It's confusing, I know, but the Changwe's cry when they're happy. I'm just beginning to figure it out myself."

Bukoba's face wrestled with the paradox of happy and sad at the same time. His compromise looked more like a smile than a grimace, so he released the door and retreated all the way to the baobab tree where he lit a cigarette. Pepsi backed away from the plane and followed him.

The sound of the Cessna's engine coming to life woke everybody as if from siestas. The pilot ran up the bank. Ngoma tossed the radio mike into the front seat of the Mercedes while Mrs. Wilson got in the back. She'd had enough. She locked herself inside and screamed.

David taxied to the end of the meadow, fiddling with knobs and levers all the way. He found the controls for the flaps and remembered how Ngoma had used them to increase the plane's lifting power. Approaching the trees, he used the control stick like a steering wheel, hoping it worked like a car. It did. It turned the nose wheel but it required extra throttle to swing the aircraft through one hundred eighty degrees. Changwe's head banged against the side window. When the plane straightened out the engine raced, propelling the aircraft forward.

David saw Ngoma driving toward him, flanked by policemen on foot.

"David!" Ngoma's voice came through speakers above David's head. "What in blazes are you doing?"

The Cessna bumped down the field at a mere thirty miles per hour. David remembered Mr. Ngoma saying a plane takes off by itself, which had to be the stupidest goddamn thing he'd ever heard. He tugged at the stick but it felt like mush.

"David! For God's sake!" The Mercedes stopped and Ngoma got out, microphone in hand.

At forty mph David pulled on the stick again. The nose lifted slightly but it cost him speed. He saw Ngoma wave his arms, his white shirt like a beacon. If he stayed where he was, he was toast, thought David. The officers knelt, rifle butts tucked into their shoulders. At fifty mph David tried again.

"Let it reach sixty, for God's sake! Sixty!"

David yanked on the stick again and this time the plane lifted off the ground but only for a second before it crashed onto its wheels, then bounced into the air. David saw policemen dive for the dirt as he blew over them, but he also saw Ngoma hold his ground with his hands together as Pepsi had done, in prayer.

It might have been prayer that helped David over the trees at the end of the meadow, or perhaps it was Ngoma's body English, his fist punching the sky.

"I have heard it said — " Ngoma came in loud and clear over the radio. "I have heard it said there comes a time when we are taken by the hand to rendezvous with destiny. I have heard of such a thing, but until now I have not entirely believed it."

David thought he heard Mrs. Wilson in the background, yelling, "You mean hijacked!" Then he was sure he heard Sergeant Bukoba insisting that it was "Angels of Mercy".

SIXTEEN

David climbed quickly, leaving behind life on the ground that now looked so minuscule. The only thing he took with him besides Mr. Changwe were Ngoma's words, particularly that bit about the rendezvous. If Ngoma had meant to say that David was lured here from halfway around the world to meet Mr. Changwe, then maybe there was something to this destiny business. Fate was something else altogether, though; now that he was flying, he had to admit a certain curiosity about miracles. David picked up the mike to say something conciliatory but Ngoma broke in first.

"David, how much petrol do you have on board?"

David reported two fuel gauges, both more than half full.

"Listen to me now," radioed Ngoma. "You're going to need three hours. It's going to be touch and — " David turned off the radio and turned to Changwe.

"He's on our side, you know that? We make it to Victoria Falls, his auntie may forgive him. After all these years."

David found a map in a door panel pocket and checked topographical features against watersheds, rivers and villages he located on the ground. As he traced with his finger along the line of the Zambezi River that marked the southern border of Zambia, the plane slipped and yawed, sometimes tilted nose-up, then sloped nose-down. But he soon got the feel of level flight.

"If that's the Luangwa, it flows into the Zambezi, Mr. Changwe. We'll follow it all the way. Or we could cut across country to save a little time."

David looked at Changwe, whose head rattled against the door.

"We're a team, Mr. Changwe, birds of a feather — I think that's what they say. We fly together."

With one hand, David pulled him upright, but where there was no longer any will, there was no way Changwe would stay put. David clenched his fist but realized he had no place to slam it without jeopardizing even keel.

"I'm sorry, Mr. Changwe! It's my fault!" He flicked on the radio.

"Come in, Cessna Charlie Victor Romeo — Charlie Victor Romeo, this is Lusaka Tower — Do you read?"

"Read my lips," David said to himself. "Save your breath." He picked up the mike and found the on-off button. He had thought of calling Lusaka when he intersected the Zambezi River but there was still far to go. Now that Lake Kariba lay beneath him, he thought of easing their minds, but then he squinted into the haze in the west and saw what looked like smoke rising off the horizon. Closer, and it looked as if it might be steam escaping from a crack in the planet.

"It's like they said, Mr. Changwe."

155

David looked wide-eyed at the approaching spectacle, a mile-wide, mist-shrouded trench that swallowed up the mighty Zambezi.

"Smoke That Thunders, Mr. Changwe!"

The rest happened in a holy silence. Though the engine roared, David's mind fell still, struck dumb by the once-in-a-lifetime spectacle of the ragged crest of the falls. On one side the broad Zambezi snaked its way from the heart of the continent. On the other side, the river churned and foamed through an odd series of lateral gorges before settling down as the meandering border between Zambia and Zimbabwe.

They made another pass, this time lower so David had a better view of the water plunging into the slash in the earth's crust. This meant passing through denser mist and surrendering to the updraft that knocked the plane around. Changwe's head fell against David's shoulder.

At the far end of the trench, David banked again, came around and made a pass even lower so that he could see the smooth texture of the dark, silent waters of the Zambezi as they approached the precipice. The glassy liquid curled over the crest and disintegrated into a billion sunstruck jewels. In the updraft the diamonds became milky with air and for a moment David lost his sense of up and down. He emerged, relieved to see that they were flying level.

Stealing a glance at Changwe, it startled David to see how empty death was of desiring or even dreaming. It felt right that here, at the heart of their destination, they should say goodbye and begin their separate journeys home to face whatever consequences the gods had in store for them.

David reached past Mr. Changwe, unlocked his door and unhooked his seat belt. He placed a hand on his friend's shoulder and squeezed gently. It took a much less gracious shove with two hands, however, to coax him out the door. The last David saw of Changwe was the stump of the leg taken by that long-ago duma who mistakenly thought that the honour was his to escort Tanzania's most dutiful son to his final resting place. In the second before the door slammed shut, a chill invaded the cockpit leaving David feeling alone and complete, tiny and huge.

He didn't fight the next strong updraft, but let the turbulence take him as high as it could, into rainbows that hovered around his plane as if he were a butterfly escaping the last shreds of his cocoon. He felt powerful and full of possibility. One of the possibilities was running out of gas. The fuel gauge for the starboard tank had been dropping and was now reading empty. David turned on the radio.

" . . . ingstone. This in Felix Fackson Ngoma. Do you read me?"

David reached for the mike to respond but Ngoma was getting frantic. "Turn on your bloody radio, man!"

"Turned on, sir. Reading you A-okay."

"For God's sake, how are you? Where are you?"

"Smoke That Thunders. I'm fine, sir. I'm turning around, heading east, I think, but I don't know how far I'll make it."

"All right, David. Air Traffic Control will give you a bearing to Kalomo. It's not far. We'll meet you there."

David turned up the volume. Although he understood Ngoma perfectly, air-space communication was another language altogether.

"Cessna Charlie Victor Romeo, this is Lusaka Tower. Do you read me?"

"Victor Romeo here," reported David.

"Good afternoon, Victor Romeo, how are you?"

"So far so good," said David. The casual approach and Scottish accent surprised him.

"That's great. What I want you to do is head zero-one-fiver degrees to Kalomo. Acknowledge that, Victor Romeo."

"Zero one five?"

"That's fifteen to you, Charlie Victor Romeo."

"Fifteen, gotcha, zero-one-five to Kalomo. No problemo." David rotated the control stick counter-clockwise and sent the Cessna into a northwards bank while Lusaka Tower ordered all other aircraft to another radio frequency.

"Charlie Victor Romeo, what's your altitude?"

"Let's see — the ALT dial says — the little needle is between three and four — thousand, I presume."

"Fine, stay at thirty five hundred feet. Your ETA will be roughly ten minutes. That's ten minutes to Kalomo, Victor Romeo. We'll stay with you all the way. We'll bring you in, Mr. Livingstone."

David was still banking northwards when the engine roared with increased revs as if it had accidentally slipped into neutral gear. David's heart skipped a beat, then pounded, as the engine coughed and, like a hay-fever victim, started missing. David clicked the mike on.

"Lusaka! I think I'm out of gas!" David could see propeller blades. You weren't supposed to see the blades, they were supposed to be an invisible whirr.

"Victor Romeo, you have two fuel gauges. What do they indicate?"

"One's empty but the other one's not! The left one's supposed to have some left!"

"Are you still banking left?"

"Yes! And I'm dropping!"

"Level out, Victor Romeo. You're sucking air on the right tank. Resume level flight and switch to your left fuel tank."

"How do I do that?"

"Black switch at the bottom of the centre column. It will be at the centre position now. Turn it all the way to the left."

A shrill blast from the stall alarm shattered David's concentration. Worse yet, the nose of the plane dropped like a roller coaster. David found the lever and jerked it left as far as it would go but the engine didn't kick in.

"I'm in a dive!" David yelled into the microphone.

"Pull back, Victor Romeo. But gently, gently, gently. You'll be gaining a lot of airspeed."

As David pulled back on the stick he began to feel the wings grab air again. The air frame vibrated as if the forces might rip the plane apart. At the same time, the engine surged with full power and, though David had lost a thousand feet, he was level again and heading north.

"Got it!" reported David. "Engine's okay! Wow, that was close."

"Charlie Victor Romeo, you scared me there, now listen up. What's beneath you?"

"A paved road, two lanes."

"Fine. Climb to four thousand and follow the road. You're on course."

He may have been on course but he wasn't sure he'd live to shiver through another sunrise. He had to land this thing.

"*Dead if you don't* is tattooed on my ass now, Mr. Changwe." David looked at the empty seat beside him. I'm talking to a dead man, he thought. A dead man who isn't even there.

"Charlie Victor Romeo, you'll see a white water tower in five minutes. Report when it's in sight."

"Okay."

David lowered the sun visor to cut the brilliant haze. He noticed something clipped behind the visor and pulled it down. It was a British Petroleum credit card in the name of Ngoma's Ministry of Highways.

"Sir David, are you there?" It was Ngoma via his car radio.

"Go ahead, Mr. Ngoma."

"You're going to land like we did at my place, David. Do you remember what we did?"

"A controlled crash. That's what you called it."

"Never mind that. I'm telling you something different now. I'm telling you that — any landing you walk away from is a damn good landing. Do you copy?"

"Roger."

"We throttled in or out for altitude, do you remember? And we pulled the nose up or down for speed. Have you got that, old chap?"

"I've got it, Mr. Ngoma. I don't think I'll ever forget it." David stuffed the BP credit card under his belt.

"Fine. Then, with a little bit of luck, my friend. With a little bit of luck."

In ten minutes, David looked down upon a dirt strip in a clearing. He saw three light aircraft tethered near a Quonset hut, a few shacks, a couple of petrol drums and a pickup truck. Clearly, no one was there to meet him. David continued to circle Kalomo at four thousand feet without reporting his arrival to Lusaka Tower. After a week on the fly he wasn't ready to touch down. He felt free and he wanted to keep it that way. He wanted to feel, for as long as he could, the lure of six more Wonders of the World just over the horizon.

"Charlie Victor Romeo, this is Lusaka Tower. Report your position."

"Lusaka Tower, this is Victor Romeo. It doesn't look like much, just an airstrip."

"That's Kalomo. Are you ready to give it a try?"

David looked at his left fuel gauge. It registered a quarter full, maybe less. How much time would that give him? Half an hour? Enough time for another start.

He pulled the credit card out from under his belt, slipped it under the clip on the visor and switched the mike on. "Lusaka, it's now or never. Let's do it."

Lusaka Tower directed David into a rectangular pattern two thousand feet above the airstrip as a practice run before lining him up and bringing him in for the real thing. He dropped the mike to concentrate with two hands on the controls because he had started to burn again. "Land like a bloody duck!" was the way Ngoma had put it, and it conjured up an image David could work with. More than that, he'd survived so much by now that he felt he must be infected with that "little bit of bloomin' luck" that

seemed to have taken such good care of Mr. Ngoma over
the years.

David soared over the runway but the thing wouldn't
touch down. He yanked the throttle all the way back and
pulled on the stick to get the damn duck's head higher but
the thing still wouldn't sit down. And now the nose blocked
his view of the runway which was quickly running out.

Bang-balloon. Bang-Balloon. Bang! Three crash land-
ings in one. The Cessna bounded towards trees at the end
of the field. He pushed hard with both feet on the rudders
as if they were brakes and, to his relief, they were. At the
end of the field he released the left rudder. The plane
swung around so that he faced the full length of the field.
David's legs shook, his knees ached and his heart pounded.
Of all his accomplishments, this ruled, yet there wasn't a
single witness as far as he could see. "Where the hell is
everyone!?" he yelled.

"Charlie Victor Romeo, Lusaka Tower. Come in, Victor
Romeo."

"I'm on the ground, Lusaka! I did it!"

"Congratulations, Livingstone. We'll have you picked up
momentarily. You'll be heading home before you know it."

Nothing moved around the hangar or at the shacks at
the far end. David taxied closer and stopped again. What
was to prevent him from helping himself to gas or even
another aircraft?

He spread maps on the passenger seat. How far were
those pyramids, anyway? He looked for Egypt but the top
edge of the map ended at the equator. He found Lake
Tanganyika and the place called Ujiji where Stanley had
finally found Livingstone, and farther south he located
Lake Bangweulu where Livingstone the Great had died of

162

jungle fever. From the little green swampy symbols on the map, it looked like a death trap.

David looked up and saw two fast-moving rooster tails of dust rising above trees beyond the end of the field. He studied the map again as if a decision was still to be made, as if this boondoggle, as Ngoma had described it, still had legs. On the top edge of the map, on the border of Tanzania and Kenya, he located Mount Kilimanjaro. The place Ernest Hemingway had written about. The Snows of Kilimanjaro. It sounded romantic enough to be an official Wonder of the World.

Three Land Rovers, one with a flashing red light on the cab, appeared from behind the Quonset hangar and sped up the runway toward him. Whatever Jackie wanted from him now, David thought, she'd have to take what she got, settle for who he was. If she couldn't live with the hole in his heart from missing his father so much, then who would? Emptiness might remain a fact of his life. Fine. The vast continent inside himself was home, at least, to a duma.

The Land Rovers fanned out to roadblock the runway. The bottom line now was that David no longer worried about what Jackie and MacGregor meant by romantic. To him it meant love of an old man and his family and the *ujamaa* of a nation that nobody back home knew much about.

The 4x4s stopped a hundred feet away, surrounding David on three sides. Zambian Police officers jumped out, seven of them brandishing pistols. David turned the ignition switch off and lifted his hands in clear surrender. The propeller fluttered to a stop. As the officers moved in on Charlie Victor Romeo, David hoped he wouldn't have to sit in the back seat next to Mrs. Wilson, fifteen hundred miles all the way back to Dar es Salaam.

Talk about a Hell Run.

.

Printed in May 1999 by
VEILLEUX
ON DEMAND PRINTING INC.

in Longueuil, Quebec